AF409799

Wayward Stars

By Clare Bohning

ALTUREZ MEDIA

Third Edition Printing August 2023

ISBN # 9798218247317

Part I
The Fleetwood Skies

For Avery, who knows it.

The Magic of Moths & Walnuts

"Oh my God, Yvonne, are you all right?!" My mother sounded frantic, but I could also hear that she was relieved I'd answered the phone.

"I'm fine, what's up?" I said groggily, wincing as I turned onto my side. I had fallen asleep on the couch. I hadn't felt like going to the bedroom, even though my legs hung over one of the couch's arms uncomfortably. My Doberman licked my face, alerted to attention when my phone rang. I shooed him off and sat up gingerly. It had been a hot drive back home that morning.

"Yvonne Daisy Meadowlark," my mother began, her voice raspy with intent. "You tell me what happened today."

"What?" I asked, totally perplexed. "I just ran errands and went and saw Grandma Lilly. What's going on?"

"I *Saw* you with a man."

"Oh God." I slapped my forehead in preparation for what was coming. My dog barked and jumped on me, knowing it was my mother on the line. He knocked my sore back into the vacuum that was somehow perched on the couch. "Ow! Mom, listen—"

"I know what happened," she insisted. She probably did, or at least sort of.

"Stop, Mom; listen."

"You were with a man at his house," she recited in the monotone timber she usually used to recite her Seeings. "You weren't wearing a shirt; not properly, anyway. He was sitting in a strange position behind you for several hours, and you were in pain! Lots of pain! I felt it in my arms and back, Yvonne!" My mother breathed in a worried, strained breath. "Please tell me you have called the police at least, baby. Don't take a shower. You sound tired. Are you all right? Tobias is on his way now."

"NO, Mom! Oh my God. Can I just tell you what happened?" I stumbled into the dark bedroom to put on a proper shirt at the mention of my brother-in-law coming to see me.

"What?" she said breathily, a mix of neutral exasperation and motherly concern. It momentarily startled me, as it was only the fifth time in my life I had heard any sort of motherly sympathy from her. It's not that she lacked it; she just seldom expressed it.

"Sit down. You won't like it," I said, looking out the window for Tobey. I called Tobias Tobey. This annoyed my sister, his wife, but Tobias was so serious that I felt it was my job to remind him, and everyone, not to take life so seriously.

My dog nipped at my free hand. I awkwardly pulled out a rawhide treat from a plastic bag and held it out for him. He took it, but his beady Doberman eyes said This doesn't mean I like it.

"I'm sitting." My mother's voice buzzed in my ear. "And I'm sure I won't like it."

"I got a big tattoo on my back," I said, awaiting the incredulous comments that were soon to follow. "The parlor is attached to the guy's house. His name is Steve. He did my other ones."

"A what? Yvonne!" she said, in both relief and exasperation. These tiny bits of motherly concern were the most affection she'd outwardly portrayed since...a few months ago. It gave me enough patience to be calm and continue.

"Yes, Mom. I got a giant tattoo on my back, which took several hours to shade and color, and it hurt like a son of a bitch." I didn't usually swear in front of my mother, but the hours under the needle that morning had made my judgment fuzzy.

"I can't believe you got another tattoo. You'll junk your body. You don't need them!"

"There's a reason I didn't tell you about it," I said. "You didn't See any of the other ones."

She sighed audibly on the other end of the line.

I leaned against the counter and drank some tea left over from the morning. I often thought what a luxury it must be for others to not have a mother who could see bits of the present and future. In my younger days, I was sometimes scolded for events that had not actually happened yet. She hadn't had those Seeings since I graduated high school—or she was tactful enough not to say anything about them. I felt bad for making my mother worry, but I was also annoyed because my back hurt and I was still tired. I waited for her to reply.

A brief silence ended with her taking in a regal breath, then her usual hard-bitten tone returned, swiftly dismissing the situation. "I'm glad you're safe, Baby Daisy." I appreciated the softer tone that probably no one else in her office could hear. "But I am very cross with you for the...art."

I grinned. My mother was far too tactful to expose my secret to her staff, though some of them already knew.

"I know, Mom. Thanks for looking out for me," I said, relieved that was all I would be hearing about it.

"You're certainly welcome. Now tell Tobias he is to return straightaway. Well, I take that back—what time is it?" One of her staff answered in the background. "That late already? Well, tell Tobias he can return if he wants to. Love you."

"Love you too," I said, getting ready to hang up.

"Oh, what did you get? I hope it's not a dragon. That is morosely déclassé," she said, returning once again to her stately self.

"No. It's Mount Shasta, with some other mountains and birds and stuff."

"Hmmm," she said thoughtfully, and I took this as the best compliment I was going to get. "Bye, Baby Daisy."

"Bye."

My phone beeped that it was low on batteries, and Silis stared at me as if to say, I told you so.

Tobias drove a Prius, which said more about him than I need describe. When it crunched onto the dirt driveway, Silis lunged to the window to bark. The car was electric blue and made the fading tan of the house look shabby. I sighed. Richard and I had planned to paint it, and I never got around to it after...things happened.

"Hi, Tobey," I said, crossing my arms over my chest. I couldn't wear a bra for the next few days at least, as the design of the mountains went right across the bra line. I've never been well endowed, but the light cotton shirt I used for pajamas was not the attire I would normally wear around my brother-in-law, or anyone, for that matter.

Tobias walked up in his pristine white pants and button-down shirt. To me, Tobias was numerical. Straitlaced and organized. All for the rules, and none for the breaking. I'd always imagined my sister marrying someone less nerdy, but Tobias was also 6' 4" and hardly out of shape.

"Good morning," he said cautiously, but I caught the indifference in his voice.

"I just talked to my mother. You can go back to work when you want," I said, though I knew he'd picked that up already from my appearance at the door. Had Mother told him about her vision? That was an embarrassing thought. I reached inside for my favorite Mt. Shasta sweatshirt. I zipped it up as he walked through my little garden. I felt much better with my favorite sweatshirt on, though I had to stand awkwardly to keep my tattoo from touching my shirt.

"You sure?" he asked unnecessarily. I heard the relief in his voice, and I felt annoyed that he had only come because of his in-law obligations. Tobias wasn't a bad person, he was just everything opposite of what I was. His pants and shirt were pressed and new. He had given me a funny look the first time we met because I was wearing jeans and a hockey shirt. I suppose he expected me to look like my sister, with a pastel sweater and perfect eyeliner.

My clothes were mostly from thrift stores, or carefully selected for their ease of movement or heartiness. I patched and redyed them when they needed it. I usually didn't wear makeup. This was the opposite of my sister, whose pride in life was her ability to look perfect for any occasion.

Tobias was the poster boy for my mother's real estate company: prompt, professional, and polite. While Tobias and my sister Darcy went out for drinks, I stayed home and drank tea out of my eclectic mug collection. They both graduated from respectable universities with master's degrees. I got an associate's degree from the local community college, which I paid for myself by working three jobs, thank you very much.

"I'm good. Thanks, though," I said.

Tobias smiled, and there was a bit of relief in the smile that reached his eyes. "It's Richard's birthday Friday," he said, catching me completely off guard. "It's August the twelfth. I believe that was Richard's birthday. Are you doing all right?"

"Yes," I managed to say, not sure if the question was meant in kindness or as a reminder. Tobias nodded, smiled, and went back to his Prius. Through the window blinds, I watched him drive away, then went to the fridge for some orange juice.

Silis was waiting for me with his leash in his mouth. It was the most comical thing I had ever seen him do, and he hadn't started doing it until Richard died.

"You want to go see Richard?" I said, in a high-pitched tone reserved for talking to dogs. Silis spun around, claws clicking on the linoleum floor. I quickly downed my glass of orange juice, clipped the extendable leash onto the dog's collar, and took a small ceramic jar off of the old radio by the stairs.

"We'll have to get some more tomorrow," I told Silis, who didn't care and scratched at the sliding glass door and looked at me like I was holding up the world.

In a weird way, I was.

I pulled the last walnut out of the ceramic jar and put it on the table to remind myself to take it with me. The jar smelled like perfume from generations past, with a strange odor of decay. That might have been because it came from Grandma Lilly's house, or because of the magic.

"Magic doesn't exist," I reminded myself. "It's just stuff that works."

I opened the sliding door and crunched out into the empty yard behind the house. It was almost sundown, and the shadows from the abundance of weeds made the backyard look particularly trashy.

"Really should tidy this up," I told the dog, who looked back at me indifferently, and then panted all the way to the back of the property, where the green 1975 Cadillac Fleetwood sat.

I had managed to keep the weeds from growing under the car.

I told Silis to sit, which he did impatiently, then unclipped his collar and opened the back door for him to jump in. Both Richard and his father would have frowned upon this, but it didn't really matter now. I looked into the front seat through the dusty window, saw a dark shadow in the passenger's seat, and made my way around to the driver's side. He must not be feeling very adventurous today.

"Hello, Richard," I said, closing the old door next to me with a click. There was nothing more satisfying than that sound. They just didn't make cars this well anymore. Richard and his father had restored it to near perfection just before Richard's dad had died from a sudden brain aneurysm.

"Hi," said the dreamy voice of the ghost sitting next to me. By "dreamy" I don't mean "swoony," I mean his voice sounded like it was sprinkled with melancholy and fairy dust while in a toilet bowl underwater. Which was very unsettling. Ghost talk creeped most people out, especially those who could not see them. I was used to it now. I had heard it every night since he had died, expect for that one time a few months ago when I went out of town and got stuck with a broken alternator.

"OK," he said vaguely. His eyes, grey now and mostly lifeless, lit up a bit at the corners when he saw me, and he smiled. It was an awkward smile, as if he had forgotten how. I smiled back and pulled the walnut out of my pocket. Before I could make it do its job, Richard's ghost hand reached out and touched my wrist.

"Is that your birthday watch?" he said. My hands almost recoiled, not because of the feeling of his touch, but because of the lack of it. I knew Richard's ghost was touching me. I knew it was pointing out the watch on my wrist and was speaking, but I could not feel him.

"Yvonne," he said without waiting for a reply. "I think we need to talk about something..."

I felt my heart sink and wished he'd go back to trying to smile. I pulled the brown walnut out of my pocket and held it out for Richard. "Here you go."

"What's this?" he said slowly.

"It's your birthday present," I lied, for the 187th time.

"I thought you forgot to get me something," said Richard. Some days he remembered the drive before the crash, some days he didn't. Today he did, which was fortunate, because I didn't know if I had the energy to invent a way to convince him to take the walnut.

I resisted the urge to scratch my hand as Silis tried to lick Richard's neck. At one point, very close to the beginning, he had been able to. It had been months since we could touch him, but the dog always tried. Richard noticed him vaguely and turned his head. The dog's snout went inside Richard's head, and Silis spent a few minutes playing "I'm going to try to snap at your brains" with Richard. Richard liked it and laughed every time Silis's face reappeared in his vision after the dog was unsuccessful at eating his brains.

I watched them for a while and felt an overwhelming sense of sadness flow over me, just for a moment—that is all I allowed. Then I swallowed it and laughed at Silis, who had his paws on the back of the seat and was vigorously snapping at Richard's transparent face. Silis's tailless butt wagged. This was his favorite part.

My favorite part had passed.

My favorite moment with Richard in the old car, with the Richard who was not really my Richard, but a ghost of what used to be, was the scant few seconds when I first got in the car and said, "Hello, Richard." For a split second, I got to imagine that he was sitting there next to me, alive, in full color, and would be able to brush my long bangs from my forehead as I fumbled with my things before we drove off. "See you in no time," he had said, before a high teenage driver had hit him in a crosswalk at 65 miles per hour.

I just needed some pain killer from the gas station, so I could drive us to see a movie.

He had been walking back to the car. I smiled at him, he smiled back, and the SUV removed him from view. To be honest, I don't remember much of what happened after that, but my mind clung to those last moments. It was the last time I saw Richard in color.

The ghost beside me was all grey, and though he laughed and played with his dog, his hands were starting to get blurry, and he couldn't remember things anymore. Every night at sunset, we sat together, Richard, Silis, and me, and watched the red sun sink behind the trees. The brush in the backyard had grown taller, and the spirit of my husband had faded.

I held out the walnut for Richard. Silis had quickly learned not to eat them. Richard took it between two ghost fingers, and delicately, as if he could see something inside the shell, he pulled out a moth. Nothing happened to the walnut. Richard looked at the moth in wonder as it fluttered about the cab. He laughed, and Silis put his head on his paws on the back of his seat, content to be with the shadow of his master.

The moth settled on the windshield, and its wings flittered to a close. Richard watched it, then saw the sky. His eyes danced at the wonder of the sunset through the windshield, and I wondered what ghosts found so riveting about the sky.

I leaned on the steering wheel so my sore back wouldn't touch the seat. I'd disconnected the car battery months ago, so I didn't have to worry about the horn. I watched the grey outline of Richard looking intently at the sunset, like he had done for so many nights before. When I squinted, it was easier to imagine he was a real person. After a while, I closed my eyes. My stinging, tattooed back was touching the cotton of my shirt, but I decided it was healed enough for a short nap.

I always knew when the sun had set because I could hear Richard say "Aaahhh…" sadly as the ghost moth disappeared. I loved and hated that sound, because it meant he was still there. I ignored the relief I felt, because it made me feel worse. He was supposed to cross over when the sun set. We had tried many different methods since the accident, but Richard was a stubborn ghost. He would not go.

"We'll have to get some more tomorrow," I told Silis. Richard was looking blankly out the window, his mouth open slightly.

"See you tomorrow, Richard," I said, and resisted the urge to kiss him on the cheek. It would just make me sadder.

Richard nodded slowly, and his eyelids fluttered, and he seemed to fall asleep. Silis harrumphed and looked out his window, waiting to be let out. I opened the Fleetwood's door carefully, wrapping my fingers around the metal edge so they would hit the neighbor's barbed wire fence before it scratched the paint Richard and his dad had spent weeks at their friend's garage applying.

I closed the door softly, though I knew no noise would wake the sleeping ghost. I let Silis out of the other side, and we both trooped back to the house. I didn't bother putting Silis's leash on, as there were no deer in sight.

I pulled out my phone and dialed the familiar numbers. Grandma Lilly answered.

"Hello?" she said. Her landline did not have caller ID.

"It's me, Gram," I said.

"Hi," she said sweetly. It was from Grandma Lilly that my mother and I had inherited our directness. Words were not often wasted.

"Hey, I need some more walnuts. He's still not gone yet."

"Not gone yet?" Grandma Lilly clicked her tongue. "And he is pulling out the moths?"

"Yep," I said. When Grandma Lilly first gave me the walnuts, she told me that after about a week, Richard would follow one away from the car with the sunset. Most ghosts did this on their own, but sometimes if their death was unexpected, it took them a while to find the sun.

No one expected Richard to become a ghost. My nerves had almost exploded when, after I parked the Fleetwood in the backyard a few days after the crash, he sort of appeared next to me. I've seen ghosts—it's my job, after all—but seeing the grey, luminous being that had once been my husband was… hard.

Richard had no interest in following the sun. Even after all the family came to see him and tried to coax him into the sunset, he remained in his car and waited for his dog to come eat his brains. Family came from overseas, specialists were called, and many baked goods were delivered to my doorstep, but nothing made Richard go with the setting sun. So, several months later, the only thing we could think to do was keep trying the walnuts, which was an old trick to lead the ghosts of children to the sun.

"Well, come by after work tomorrow and I'll get you some more," said Grandma Lilly kindly. After so many months, people had stopped asking about him, and I'd stopped talking about him. It was hard enough for everyone else to lose him; I was getting tired of seeing the sadness and pity in their faces when the topic arose. Grandma Lilly was kind and only brought it up if I did.

"I just Saw something," said Grandma Lilly. I waited as she recollected her Seeing. "There is a house they will want you to help with tomorrow. You'll have to go. You can pick up the walnuts afterwards."

I groaned, because Grandma Lily, unlike Mom, was usually accurate in her Seeings. I had taken the next few days off to let my tattoo heal and get some work done around the house. The first would happen; the second was now questionable.

We said our goodnights and hung up. Silis was waiting for me by the back door. He whined at my tardiness.

"Come on, buddy, we have to get up early for work tomorrow."

Silis trotted into the house.

I had to get up to lock the screen door and turn off the stove before I fell asleep, because I had forgotten them both.

Ghosts of Grumpy

I got a call from Tobias at 8 a.m. Mother wanted my help with a house they hadn't been able to sell. Meadowlark Real Estate Specialists was an all-in-one realty and home design agency, specializing in getting unattractive and long-for-sale properties to sell. Mom owned the company, Janis and Tobias were head Realtors, and Mark and Darcy were head home designers. Mom and I dealt with the tricky ones.

Silis and I rolled up to a particularly rickety place just past 9:30 in the morning. Mom was already there, sipping her expensive coffee, black, with no lid. Her large sunglasses covered her face. In her other hand was a novel, of the paperback supernatural romance variety.

"No wonder she thought I was doing dirty things," I told Silis, pulling the keys out of the Trooper's worn ignition. Silis jumped out of the passenger's seat and sat patiently. He knew it was work time, so he was a lot more patient than he had been last night.

We trotted up the gravel drive to Mom, who set her coffee on the hood of her convertible but did not put the book down until Silis rubbed his side along her knee-length coat.

"Silis!" she pronounced. The dog was unfazed and waited patiently for her to give him attention. She begrudgingly gave it after tucking her frilly bookmark in between pages. It was a handmade bookmark with a rainbow-braided ribbon. My niece Stephanie had made it for her, and though it completely clashed with her convertible and designer clothes, it was never farther than her latest romance novel, which was never far.

"You're late," she said.

"You got a chance to read more," I said.

I really wasn't that late, and I felt I had a good excuse, because it was my day off. I had to stand up awkwardly straight to keep my tattoo from rubbing against my shirt. I also hadn't worn my nicer work clothes, which made me look like a disheveled college student instead of a disheveled bum. I was wearing my Mt. Shasta sweatshirt and one of the sweaters Grandma Lilly made for me. It was supposed to get hot later, but it had been cold when I got up.

Silis, satisfied with the light scratch on the head from my mother's gloved hand, trotted up to the house and started sniffing everything, all business. My mother took a meaningful look at my appearance and rolled her eyes, but gave me a kiss on the cheek; then her attention went to business, too. "This is the 88 Willow Road property."

"Sounds creepy," I said.

"Not really. It's just been on the market for a long time." She took out her key for the Realtor box and pushed the door open. There was a great big lawn that looked out over some green fields. It was a pretty spot, prettier than I'd thought it would be, considering the neighborhood. Aside from the neglect from several months on the market, it was quite cute.

Mom cleared her throat at the door, distracting me from the view. We crossed the threshold, and Silis sniffed everything from the old mint-colored carpet to the couch Darcy had put there to make the room seem more inviting.

I never understood the point of decorating a home to be sold. Were some people so unimaginative that they needed chairs and dressers and beds that wouldn't even come with the house to figure out if they liked it? Apparently they did, because it was a big part of the business.

Mom sat down on the couch and reclined like a diva in a '20s black and white film. She closed her eyes, tilted back her head, and sighed. The couch had a remarkable view across the sunny fields and tall wildflowers growing outside.

Silis sniffed around, his claws clicking when he entered the linoleum kitchen. Then the sniffing stopped, and I heard the telltale sounds of Silis lying down.

I walked into the kitchen, which still had a framed embroidery flower hanging in it, dust and spider webs trapped behind it. I wondered why Darcy had chosen to leave this piece behind. Darcy always left something of the original house.

It kept the ghosts happy.

Silis was lying on the cool linoleum. He looked up at me with big brown eyes as I approached, then put his head down between his paws, looking into the bedroom beyond the refrigerator.

I opened one of the cabinets to see if there were any cups left. There was one, an old Christmas mug with a jolly Santa on it. It smelled like hard water and a rundown water heater. Darcy had probably left this for me, too, a nod to my collection of gaudy Christmas mugs. Sometimes there was dirt and spiders in cups she left behind. This one looked pretty clean.

I pulled it out and closed the cabinet, then filled the mug with water from the metal sink. I wasn't going to drink it unless this ghost was particularly stubborn. Ghosts were funny things, usually existing as only the habitual parts of themselves. The real soul went on, with the rare exception like Richard.

The sound of opening a cupboard, taking out a cup, and filling it with water was unique to every house, and something most everyone did. The sound provoked the remnant ghost to appear. At least, it usually did.

Silis let out a low "Ruff." I leaned casually against the counter. Silis sat up sharply. I turned around, and the grey shadow of an old man was right in my face.

"Quit slammin' the cupboards!" he yelled, which really was only a whispering echo. He was an old ghost and had probably died several years ago; there wasn't much left.

"Ah, man," I said, and put the cup down on the counter. Silis sat on my feet, in between me and the ghost, which made it impossible to move.

"This ain't no Motel 6! This is my home! You are a disgrace!" The last words trailed off. The old man's shadow disappeared for a moment.

After a few minutes of silence, I called out, "Mom, it's a grumpy one!"

I heard Mom grumble, and I pictured her putting her freshly manicured fingers on her forehead.

"Do you think he'll go with the noon sun?" she called. The sun at noon and dawn were also times spirits could leave, but they weren't as powerful as a setting sun.

Something out the window caught my eye. I could barely make out the grey silhouette in the shadow of the trees, but there was no mistaking that the old man was storming around and fuming about the state of his garden hose.

"Nope," I said. Silis gave me a dirty look as I pushed him off my feet. "But he's in the garden. You can banish him now."

"Oh, good," I heard, and I knew she would be making a "claim." The books my mother read made a big deal about ghosts being vicious, and salt and enchantments and stuff, when really all it took to get a ghost to leave was to tell them to, and mean it. I heard Mom speaking in the kitchen. "This house belongs to Meadowlark Real Estate Specialists. You are welcome someplace other than here. Do not trespass again." My mother said this authoritatively, like a judge laying down a sentence. Ghosts responded to this pretty well: if you said it with enough meaning, they usually got the message and moved on. Mom had the speech down to a science.

I heard gravel crunch in the driveway.

"Darcy and Tobias are here," called Mom. "Is Mr. Grumpy still around?"

I watch as Mr. Grumpy stomped across the back yard to the Prius. "Yep."

My mother groaned and gathered herself to leave. "It's going to be one of those days."

Silis barked when he heard the Prius's door close. Mom went out the door to meet Darcy and Tobias, and I clicked on Silis's leash. "I'll go talk to him," I said.

"It might help," Mom said thoughtfully.

She immediately began talking to Darcy about some business with another big sale that morning. Darcy's bleached hair was immaculately coiffed, and her pink lipstick flashed as she spoke quickly. Tobias was tying his shoe and almost fell over when Silis ran over to lick his face.

Tobias was still trying to dissuade the eager dog when Mr. Grumpy came up next to him and started yelling.

"You dirty rotten kids! You can't park here! Get off my property! Take that lousy piece of imported trash out! OUT!" The threats would have been ear shattering if he had not been quite so dead.

Tobias couldn't see ghosts, though he was sensible enough to believe that what Mom and I did to houses caused them to sell. I winced at the insults. Tobias scratched his ear. When he got up, he looked tired. Mr. Grumpy tried to tap him hard on the shoulder.

"Hey, hey! I'm talking to you!" the ghost shouted.

Tobias swatted at his shoulder as if a mosquito had bitten him. Mr. Grumpy looked aghast.

"Hi, Yva," said Darcy, and she pecked me on the cheek. She was the only person I knew who greeted people like that. "How are you?"

"Good, how are you all?" I asked.

"Good. Stephanie is practicing her guitar with Mr. Graves. Jasper is spending most of his time in his tree house and with that video game you got him." She said the last part dryly.

"It's almost summer break. He's got time to play video games," I said. Silis came up and sat like a good Doberman in front of Darcy. Darcy petted his head. Silis only behaved this well with Darcy, as if her regality mirrored some part of his regal heritage.

"How are you, Mr. Silis?" she said, in high-pitched dog talk. Silis licked her hand. "Good boy," she said "I wish Grop was this well behaved. Want to trade?" she said, half joking. Grop was their bulldog mutt from the pound. Jasper had named him, and it fit his personality very well.

Darcy and I spoke briefly about the house and how I must come to dinner Friday night before Mother whisked her away into the house.

"Ow!" said Tobias, holding a coffee cup with a misplaced lid. He was wiping off the spilled coffee on his dark shirt. "Hot hot hot."

"Bummer," I said. Silis licked the coffee off Tobey's burned hand, which he tolerated, then he wiped it on the grass after the dog deemed him clean. Mr. Grumpy was furious.

Tobias walked slowly to the door. He had dark circles under his eyes and radiated a level of melancholy not usual to his personality.

"You OK?" I asked.

"Yeah, just feel a little worn out today." He smiled briefly, which was really just his lips tightening, and went into the house with Darcy. Mr. Grumpy was trying to lift the Prius off the grass.

"How is our friend?" asked Mom. Mr. Grumpy was now jumping on the roof of the car, screaming like Tarzan.

"He's not going anywhere," I said.

"Hmmm," said Mom. "At least he can't get back in the house. You better go see Grandma Lilly. Meet you back here tonight?"

"Sure. See you. Bye Tobey, bye Darce."

I walked past Mr. Grumpy, who was now trying to pull the hose over from the backyard, presumably to hit the Prius with, but having no success.

Silis jumped in the back seat, and I put the air-conditioning on as we drove down the obscure road to my Grandma Lilly's.

"Hi there," said Grandma Lilly. I came in through the back door because the front was covered in thick, beautiful rose bushes, which meant they were entrenched with spiders. Grandma Lilly was in the back anyway, taking some laundry out of the little sunroom with the stacked washer/dryer.

"Hi, Gram," I said. Silis was in the car with the windows down, under a shady tree. I didn't want to keep him there long. But Grandma Lilly always had some baking or other going on and usually had a crumb or two on her floral apron, and Silis couldn't resist jumping on her to eat them.

"I smell ginger," I said.

"Yes," said Grandma Lilly. "I was drying some for tea. You need some walnuts?"

"Yep yep," I said. Grandma Lilly led the way to the living room and attached kitchen, which was a lovely space, full of things for cooking and comfortable places to sit. There was a loaf of zucchini bread in plastic wrap with a butter dish next to it. I cut myself a piece and slathered it with butter as Grandma delicately collected some walnuts from an enormous jar by the potatoes. The walnuts clapped together as they fell, one by one, into a small paper sack. I had forgotten to bring the jar.

"There." She folded up the top and placed the sack on the counter.

"Oh, can I have a couple extra? Mom wants some for a client."

Grandma Lilly sighed, but put her hand in the jar for a few more. "I don't know why she doesn't get her own. It's not like they are hard to come by."

"I think you are the only one she knows who buys them in bulk," I said, savoring the warm, sticky zucchini bread. The butter she got was always soft and spreadable, like frosting. When I was little, I dreamed of having a butter dish like Grandma Lilly's, so I could put soft butter on everything. That still hadn't happened.

"It's just the supermarket," she said, and put the extra walnuts in the paper sack. "Oh good, you found the zucchini bread. Where are you off to?"

"Nowhere in particular," I said, resisting the urge to scratch my back. The tattoo was still sore, but the lesser lines were healing, which meant they were starting to itch. In truth, I planned to go home and take a shower, then nap until it was late enough to give Richard his walnut.

"Can I ask you a favor?" Grandma Lilly asked, tilting her head. I swallowed the bread and took a tall water glass out of the old cabinet.

"Sure, what's up?"

Grandma Lilly folded her hands on the counter, hands that were old and wrinkled but still strong. "You remember Matilda?"

"Yes," I said. Matilda was Grandma Lilly's neighbor—or at least, had been her neighbor. Matilda had died of a terrible cancer a few weeks before.

"She's still in the garden," said Grandma Lilly, pointing to the overgrown backyard that she shared with a few of the neighbors. "You think you could talk to her?"

"Um," I said.

"I know you don't want to. That's OK. I'm sure she'll figure it out, but I think she's disturbing the growth of the raspberries."

"I'll go talk to her. I just can't stay long because Silis is in the car."

"No problem, Baby Daisy," she said. Only Mom and Grandma called me Baby Daisy, and as far as I was concerned, they were the only ones with the right to. I smiled and drained my glass of water. It was well water, ice cold and delicious.

"I'll be right back."

I hopped off the back porch into the sun. It was very bright out, which always gave me a headache, but the wind was cool, which helped. Silis's head lay on the windowsill of my car, his eyes half open, nostrils idly sniffing something on the wind. I walked around to the back of the house, avoiding any tall branch that might house an unhappy spider.

Matilda was indeed there, sitting on the cement block wall by the raspberries, almost hidden in the trees. The leaves were rustling so much I could hardly hear my feet touch the ground.

She saw me approach and smiled, then she tapped the stone next to her, and I sat, but not before making sure there were no creepy crawlies on it.

It was a little quieter there, as the wall blocked the wind. The sun blinked at me through layers of leaves, and I folded my hands in my lap. Since she was so responsive to my presence, I figured it would be all right to talk first.

"What's up, Matilda?" I said. I learned a while ago that it was a bit rude to ask a ghost, "How are you?" But the casual greeting was pretty interpretable, and modern ghosts were mostly receptive to it.

Matilda's grey form breathed in the garden and did not respond right away. I wondered if she could smell the garden, or if, as a ghost, she could smell it differently. Did dead flowers leave a ghost smell? It seemed impolite to ask, so I let the question lie.

"I wanted to say something to you," she said, pulling one knee up to her chest. "I wasn't sure if you could actually see me. I know you used to talk to yourself when you were really little. I'd watch you when you were out here in the far garden, to make sure you didn't fall off the high stones. You'd be talking away like there were fifty others there. But it was just you, and sometimes your sister. But you never talked to her like you talked to us."

"What do you want to tell me?" I asked. Sometimes ghosts could ramble, and even though it was fairly pleasant in the old garden, I wanted to get Silis out of the car.

Matilda sighed and put her hands on the stones next to her, as if she was getting ready to leave.

"I wanted to talk to someone about... something I felt when I was dying. I couldn't speak at the end." She put her hand on her throat. "It got too bad. But there was something I realized at the end, and I wanted to tell someone. I'm kind of embarrassed, but I'm dead, so I don't care."

Her grey eyes looked right at me, and she said, "The worst part was the sex."

"What?" I said, and I swear I almost fell off the wall. I didn't talk about sex at the most comfortable of times, and talking with a ghost about it seemed surreal.

"Yeah. Not like it was bad or anything. It was just... Dwayne and I, we did it all the time. It was ordinary. The last time we did it before I got diagnosed... When I was sick, I kept thinking back to that last time, and it just seemed so ordinary. There were things I wish I had done different, but the one thing I wish I would have done was screwed him like I loved him, every single time. So there would have been no time for ordinary. I should have seen it coming. I guess I never really thought that there would be a last time. I thought that there would always be another time to hold him close and have him feel how much I loved him. Do you think he knew how much I loved him?"

I couldn't say anything for a bit. Her words hit me somewhere I didn't think they could, but I nodded. "Yeah," I said. It came out quieter than I'd expected, so I cleared my throat and said, louder, "I bet he did."

Matilda nodded. "Thanks. I just...wanted to tell somebody. Seems like something no one thinks to say."

Matilda looked back over the garden. Suddenly her eyes caught the reflection of the sun and they shone, and for a minute I thought she was going to go to the sun, but then the wind rustled, and she blinked. Then she rubbed her ghost shoulders and smiled at me again. "I guess I'm rambling. You better go check on your grandmother. It's the living you need to be watching out for."

I left the backyard, went inside, and grabbed the bag of walnuts off the kitchen counter. I told Grandma Lilly about Matilda, and she pursed her lips and said, "Hmmm."

I drove Silis back to our house, where I planned to take a shower before going back to the house with Mr. Grumpy. I had never been a Future Seer, but I could always see ghosts. It got more prevalent when Richard died. After the accident, I quit my good day job at the bookstore and started talking to ghosts for a living. The world had changed so fast...

Distracted by my thoughts, I almost didn't see Mr. Grumpy running across the road.

I slammed on the brakes, but not hard enough to disturb Silis too much. My car went right through Mr. Grumpy, and I watched as he ran down the sidewalk, turning my way and cursing before running back down the road again. A truck honked behind me and I drove on, but chose to turn off at my sister's house instead of going straight to mine, which was no doubt Mr. Grumpy's destination.

Guitars & Cheese

"HI, YVA!" shouted Jasper from his tree house overhanging the driveway.

"Hey, Crazy!" I called to my eleven-year-old nephew. He scampered down the tree branches as quick as a squirrel. Tobias's blue Prius took up a significant portion of the driveway, considering its size, and I had to maneuver my car just right to avoid parking on the grass.

Jasper roared and pummeled me with a hug. He was getting big, almost as tall as my chin, but I could still pick him up off his feet, so I did. My back was not happy about it, but I ignored it.

Grop waddled out of the house and barked in alarm. When he recognized who we were, he licked his large chops and leaned his entire weight against my leg until I had sufficiently scratched his back. Then he wandered back into the house and flopped down on his expensive dog bed to sleep.

Through Jasper's detailed account of his progress in his latest video game, I could hear Darcy and Stephanie arguing in the kitchen.

"What's up?" I asked Jasper.

He shrugged. "Something about a guitar breaking and her not wanting to fix it. I'll meet you upstairs."

"Oh, sorry, buddy, I can't play today. I have to go do some work with my mom and your mom," I said with the regret I felt.

Jasper's shoulders slumped in disappointment, but he smiled. "I'll just show you my character. Come up before you go."

"Deal," I said, shaking his hand in honor. Jasper ran upstairs, and I went into the kitchen. My niece, Stephanie, was fifteen and believed she knew better than what her mother had to say, but still wanted help with almost everything. Darcy was a middle-aged woman who had her act together and knew her place in the world. They argued a lot. Neither of them was usually completely wrong, but the way they spoke to each other created sparks, causing the smallest things to end in fireworks.

Darcy was standing behind the kitchen island. A shiny guitar was lying on it. Two of the strings had snapped, and one of the tuning pegs was broken.

"I told you not to do anything with it until your instructor told you to do so!" said Darcy.

"It was an accident!" said Stephanie, and I could tell these two points had probably been argued for at least half an hour. "I was doing fine; something was wrong with the strings."

"There was nothing wrong with these strings," said Darcy, picking up one of the snapped strings and the broken peg for emphasis. "This doesn't happen from a simple malfunction. This was done because you messed with it without knowing what you were doing."

"Mr. Graves showed me how to do this!" said Stephanie.

"When?" Darcy asked.

"Two weeks ago!" said Stephanie, but the slight hesitation in her voice made her lose her conviction. I heard it, and so did Darcy, who set the peg back on the table, then turned back around and saw me for the first time.

"Yvonne! I'll be right out," she said. "Don't touch this until Mr. Graves tells us how to fix it," she told Stephanie.

"I won't break it anymore!" cried Stephanie.

"I said no! That was a very expensive instrument, Stephanie. You need to be respectful of the gifts people give you." And with that, Darcy went into the other room, ending the conversation with a snap of the door.

Stephanie exclaimed in frustration and started crying. "I didn't mean to do it," she said softly, looking up at me remorsefully through heavily mascaraed eyes. She grabbed a paper towel and wiped makeup off her smeared face. Her hair was done up all nice too and she was wearing very elegant clothes. She must have been in her room, rehearsing for a far-off concert, when the strings broke.

"Why don't you go change? I'll have a look at it," I said, picking up the guitar. Stephanie nodded and wiped her eyes with the back of her hand as her high heels clopped down the hardwood hallway. She was still not quite used to wearing them.

"You better not be scuffing up the hardwood with those shoes, Stephanie!" Darcy called from the other room.

Stephanie stamped and shouted "UUUUUUGGGHH!!!" and ran up the stairs. I heard her trip partway up and the door slam shut a moment later.

Darcy marched back in, fussing with her pearl earrings and straightening her scarf. "That girl," she said. Then she looked at the guitar I was inspecting and sighed. "I'm sorry about the guitar. She can pay you back if you want. I know it was one of Richard's favorites."

"It's fine," I said, inspecting the broken peg and the snapped strings.

"No, it's not fine. She should have been more careful with something so precious, especially since you gave it to her from Richard." She took a small red-wax-covered ball of cheese from the fridge and tossed one on the counter for me. I snatched it and put it in my pocket for later. It was my favorite cheese.

"It's all right," I said, in the same patient, neutral tone I used to talk to ghosts. "Richard wanted her to have it. It wasn't his best one either. I'm glad she's using it and likes it." I plucked on a few strings to distract Darcy from retorting, as I knew Stephanie could hear us. No one else seemed to notice that Stephanie could hear what happened in the house, or they ignored it, which I sometimes felt was a great injustice to my clever niece. Jasper, not so much. He usually didn't care enough to listen. "It won't take much to fix it. I can take it in tomorrow to have it restrung. I can bring over another one until it's finished."

"Well, we'll see about that," said Darcy, sounding relieved that I wasn't hurt.

"I should have been here to teach her," I said, playing a few notes on the remaining strings. They were, to Stephanie's credit, in tune. "I haven't been around enough."

"It's all right, but we should go. We have a work party to attend afterward as well. I forgot to ask you, could you watch the kids tonight?"

"Sure," I said. I'd already guessed that would be the case. They didn't really need watching, it was just that none of us liked them being home alone.

"They'll be thrilled," said Darcy. She called to Tobias and went to wait in the car. I spotted Stephanie looking down at me from upstairs. I smiled at her and mouthed "It's fine" while pointing to the guitar and giving her a thumbs-up. She smiled and went back to her room.

Jasper came thumping down the stairs next and practically dragged me up to see the progress of his game character.

Fifteen minutes later, after a rapid and thorough discussion about hero stats and appropriate weapons for fighting the dead, I was back in the front yard. Darcy was checking her email on her phone while talking to Tobias in the Prius. I waved and got my keys ready to go. Silis barked at me for taking so long.

"Sorry, buddy, but Jasper was defending the kingdom," I explained.

I pulled out of the driveway first, but not before noticing there was someone else sitting in the Prius, and I almost ran into a passing car. The driver honked and I waved, embarrassed. Darcy and

Tobias looked concerned, but Mr. Grumpy, sitting in between them, looked right furious at Tobias.

"Hmmm. I don't think they are going to make it to the party tonight, Silis."

I pulled out of the driveway and called Mom on speakerphone.

"Hi, Mom," I said, talking loudly so the speaker would pick it up.

"Are you talking while driving?" she asked sternly.

"It's on speaker on my dashboard," I said. With voice recognition technology, I could turn it on and off with a command. I had left my Bluetooth headset at home. "Listen, I think Mr. Grumpy is haunting Tobias, and Grandma Lilly's old neighbor Matilda won't cross over either."

"Hmmm." Her voice buzzed, and I had to push Silis back to keep him from trying to eat the phone. I knew better than to call this way, but it felt necessary, and we were still in the slow-going, crowded neighborhood. I continued, saying what Mom probably already suspected.

"The sun isn't getting them to leave. We're probably going to have to do a moon crossing."

"Hmmm," my mother said again.

"I'm leading Darcy and Tobias to the firm. I'll see you there in a few minutes."

"All right, bye." The dial tone clicked, and Silis relaxed. In the rearview mirror, I could see Tobias looking at me strangely, but he soon figured out where we were going when I took the fastest route to the office.

The Light of Mirrors

"A moon crossing?" said my younger sister, Janis. She had her hair done up in large, purple curls today, and her glasses were bright orange, as was her lipstick. "Hey, Mark, where's your iPad?" she called to a back office.

"Where's yours?" Mark called back.

"At home on the charger," said Janis.

"Of course it is," said Mark. He appeared a bit later, wrapping a cord around an orange case. He waved to me.

"Hi, Yvonne! Nice Shasta sweatshirt." He gave me a double thumbs-up and went back to work in the other room. He was several years younger than Janis, but they didn't seem to mind. At first I thought Mark's overzealous gestures were flirtatious, then I realized he was just an outgoing young man with a short attention span. They seemed to complement each other very well, which was fortunate, because Janis was pregnant. Her orange shirt protruded fashionably from under her sharp blazer.

Janis typed something on the iPad faster than I knew how to. She had gone to some fancy tech university and worked part time as a data librarian. She was considered a part-time real estate agent, but Tobias did most of the realty work. Janis ran the computers and the databases but had a particular flair for certain types of customers who were looking for an eclectic homestead.

"What exactly do we need to do to do a moon crossing?" asked Tobias, who was sniffling as if he had a cold. Mr. Grumpy was standing just two inches from him, fuming and shouting insults that I had long ago tuned out. I had tried to get him off Tobias when we got to the office, but the old fart wouldn't pay any attention to me, and the negative energy was starting to really mess with Tobias.

"Well, you have to have the sun shining in darkness," said Janis, "which in olden times was a tricky thing to do. I think somewhere in history, they tried this elaborate mirror technique, or paintings of suns. Now we have tablets and YouTube, and this shit's way easier."

"Ahem," said Mother.

"Sorry," said Janis at our mother's disapproval of her foul language.

"What do tablets do?" asked Darcy. She didn't have much to do with our work, but her husband's health was concerning her enough to make her curious—curiosity she'd never had as a child.

"We find a live feed of the sun, or a video or a picture of the sun, and point it at the sky. The best is sunsets," said Janis, grabbing her messenger bag. "Mark! Don't forget hot dogs and marshmallows!"

"You got it," called Mark.

"Thank you!" said Janis as we all headed out the door.

"Are you having a barbeque tonight, Janis?" asked Darcy.

"Yeah. Don't worry, I got veggie burgers this morning for you and Stephanie," said Janis.

"Oh, I didn't know. Um, Tobias and I are going to the open house tonight—"

"No, you won't be," said Janis, without looking up from her device. Somehow she didn't run headlong into my car. "We're going to pick up Matilda at Gram's, get Richard from Yvonne's, and Tobias will take Mr. Grumpy and the kids with him to the cemetery." Janis tapped her orange glasses and said in a singsong voice, "I Saw it."

She plopped herself into the passenger's seat of my Trooper and occupied herself with the tablet. Silis behaved himself enough not to jump in her lap.

I froze. Mom put her arm on my elbow. I swallowed. Part of me said, Yes, it's time. Another part of me wanted to run away and keep Richard in my backyard forever, though I knew, devastatingly, that what was floating in the Fleetwood out back was not my real husband.

"Takes a bit of the plot out of the story, doesn't it? But it can't be helped. Better get going, I suppose," blustered Darcy. "Can I borrow some clothes from your house, Yvonne?"

"Sure," I said, without much thought. Mom hopped in as well. Any other day, I would have been self-conscious about the burrito wrappers on the floor, the empty iced tea cups in the cup holders, and the copious amounts of dog hair, but today, I wasn't. My brain had a fuzzy quality, and I felt a burning panic building deep in my stomach. I had to keep it at bay.

I vaguely watched Darcy give Tobias a kiss, then squeeze herself into the back seat of my Trooper with Mom. Tobias had to close the door of the Prius twice. He seemed to think his seat belt had been in the way, but my bet was on Mr. Grumpy trying to rip the door off.

It was a tight fit in my car, and everyone was happy to hop out when we reached my house. In the light before nightfall, it looked even more disheveled.

Janis even whistled at the mess.

I unlocked the door and pushed laundry and unsorted recycling out of the way with my foot. The rest of the house didn't look much better. Part of me wanted to say I had taken the next few days off to clean, but I couldn't form the words with my mouth; they fell out before becoming full.

I found a clean-clothes basket and handed Darcy some clothes. To my surprise, she took my old hiking shorts and Wonder Woman T-shirt without hesitating, going into the spare bedroom to change.

My back felt disgusting.

"Janis, could you help me wash my back?" I asked.

"Wash your back?" she said. "Why?"

"She got a tattoo," said Mother, perched artfully on the only clean barstool. "I'm sure it feels miserable," she added.

I gave her a look, but was secretly glad to feel something other than the freefalling sensation in the pit of my stomach.

"Oooooh!" said Janis. "What'd you get?"

"It's a scene with Mount Shasta, some trees and stuff."

"Oh, cool. Sure, I'll help you." said Janis, and winked when Mom wasn't looking. I was secretly envious of Janis, who sported a giant forest scene with a puma on her back. Just my luck my tattoo would be the one that Mother Saw.

Janis followed me into the bedroom, which was, happily, cleaner than I'd thought.

"Do you want to change too?" I asked her.

"Hmmm." She looked down at her business—but adorable—attire. "Yeah, sure. Better keep these nice for work."

I gave her some options from another clean-clothes basket and went into the attached bathroom to undress. I washed my face quickly but did not look at myself. I couldn't do that, not yet.

I brought out a clean roll of paper towels that Janis would have to carefully dry my tattoo with and a brand-new soft, fluffy towel. I had gotten the towels a few weeks ago from Darcy, who had bought all-new ones to fit the color scheme of her house. I let the water run for a minute behind the curtain and got in when it was warm enough to bear, but not hot enough to inflame the tattoo. I carefully washed my hair.

I heard a knock on the door and Janis stepped in, closing the door behind her. She was wearing my red Smokey Bear shirt and a pair of cutoff shorts I rarely wore, but which fit her perfectly. "You ready?" she said.

"Yep," I said.

She washed her hands in the sink, and then I poured unscented soap into her cupped hands from behind the curtain. I turned the showerhead to the wall to keep it from spraying Janis and turned my back to her.

"Oooo!" she said. "That's very pretty! Did Steve do it?" Her hands were gentle when she rubbed the sore spot on my back Steve had spent hours laboring over the previous day.

"Yeah. He says hi," I said, splashing warm water on my front to keep from getting cold.

"Did he design it?"

"No, I did."

"What?" said Janis, inspecting it more carefully. "Yvonne, this is beautiful! Not just pretty, but well designed. Did you pick out the colors too?"

"No, he did most of the color."

"Still." She motioned for the showerhead. I pulled it off the rack and handed it to her. "You should start drawing again. You could get a job as an illustrator, easy."

"It's harder than it seems," I said.

"Yvonne, this is amazing art. And I'm not just saying that because I'm your sister and this is permanently tattooed on your skin. You know what this reminds me of? That picture you drew on my cap at graduation. Do you remember?"

"Oh, yeah." I remembered the rebellious puma I had hastily drawn on her cap before they walked. Seniors weren't supposed to decorate their caps, but Janis wanted to anyway, and I was happy to help.

"You've seen the one I have on my back, right?" said Janis.

"I think so. It's the puma, right?"

"Yes, Steve based it off your drawing."

"Really?" I said.

"Yes."

"I didn't know that."

"It was a few months ago, right after the...crash." There was a pause as she gently rubbed away the last of the dead skin and leftover ink that would come off today. "It didn't seem like the right time to tell you."

"You know the strangest part about Richard being gone?"

"What?" asked Janis quietly.

"There was no one here to wash my back." It was the most I had spoken to another person about Richard since the crash. I quickly washed my hair again to disguise my sudden tears. Janis rinsed off the soap.

"We're here, you know," she said. "We've always been here."

"Yeah," I said, feeling the free fall start in the pit of my stomach again. "I know."

What I couldn't tell her was that it was not the same.

Janis patted my back dry with paper towels and spread some unscented lotion lightly over the tattoo. I would have waited a little longer to do this, but it was hot out and I didn't want it to get too dry.

I changed into my almost completely faded Batman shirt and dark knee-length shorts. I got cold easily and usually never wore shorts above my knees.

Mom was reading her romance novel when I came out, and the room was miraculously organized. Mom was a miracle cleaner. Sometimes I wondered if it was a gift, like seeing bits of the future or talking to ghosts. If so, I certainly hadn't gotten it.

"So, do you think the moon crossing will work tonight?" I asked Mom as I grabbed the keys to the Fleetwood.

Mother looked pensive. "Should…"

Silis trotted out the sliding door first. The evening had barely grown cooler, and crickets were chirping. It was going to be a warm night.

Everyone stopped a good distance from the old Cadillac Fleetwood. Silis and I went ahead. I opened the back door for Silis. He jumped in and shook dirt all over the back seat. I suddenly remembered how spotless the car used to be. I had really let it go. I closed the door, hooked up the battery, and made my way to the driver's seat.

Somehow I knew he was in the passenger's seat, waiting for me.

I clicked open the driver's-side door, putting my fingers between the metal and the barbed wire. I never once hit the barbed wire, and neither did the door.

"Hello, Richard," I said, and slid into the driver's seat. I fumbled with my keys and let the moment drag on, trying not to breathe in the musty smell of the abandoned car as I pulled out the ignition key in the yellow sunset. Something inside me fluttered. This was the last time. I didn't want it to be the last time.

Richard's grey hand touched my wrist. I looked up, and for the first time in months, he looked lucid.

"Yvonne, we have to go." The dreamy voice said more than the words could. I gulped, nodded, and turned the key. The old luxury car was surprisingly quiet considering the big engine I knew was inside it.

I met Richard's grey eyes, eyes that had once been blue. He gave me one last, encouraging look, and I pulled forward so my sisters and mother could get in with us.

Lost Ghosts

It didn't take long to get to Grandma Lilly's house. Matilda had gotten in the back of the Fleetwood with Darcy and Silis. She had always had her eye on it, but was too shy to ask for a ride, she confided. Richard sat in the front between me and Mom.

My mother owned a real estate company based off of banishing ghosts, my sister, mother, and grandmother could see the future, and my dog and I could see ghosts. All this strangeness, but all I could think about was Richard sitting next to me.

Janis and Grandma Lilly were crowding into Gram's little green mini coupe to join us at the cemetery. I watched Gram dial a number on her ancient cellphone.

My phone rang, and it took a while for me to pry it loose from under the seat. "Hello?"

"Hi, Baby Daisy, it's Grandma," she said unnecessarily.

"Hi, Gram, what's up?"

"Nothing you'll like, I'm afraid," she said seriously. "I just Saw something, but it's not going to be good for you."

"What is it?" I asked, scratching Silis behind the collar.

Gram's voice took on the rhythmic tone she used when relating a vision. "You need a relic to transport the reluctant."

"Yes, we have the Fleetwood." Transports had to be picked with care. A hearse worked because they were ceremonially used at funerals. A carriage worked because they were usually handmade and repaired with care. The Fleetwood had not only been made in an era when cars were built with more style than today, but Richard and his dad had spent years restoring it. It was the epitome of a transport vehicle. "Matilda and Richard attached to it right quick. It should work. That should be everything, right?"

"Not quite," said Grandma Lilly. "This moon is a tricky one. There is something else we need. Are you ready?"

"Yes, I'm ready," I said, sure that nothing could be harder than finally seeing my husband depart forever.

"You need to find Lewis and take him too," she said, and hung up. I kept the phone to my ear long after it clicked. I finally handed it to Mom, through Richard's shadowy ribcage. She took it and called Grandma Lilly back, because my ears were ringing and I couldn't hear her.

I drove to the last place I wanted to go, and somehow didn't get pulled over in the process.

"Lewis!" I called, slamming the Fleetwood's door. The word sounded harsh in my ears. If anyone had been around, they would have thought it strange that a grown woman was yelling at a garbage can behind a gas station, because they probably would not have been able to see the ghost of the skinny, disheveled kid who sat on it. The ghost scratched his grey head but did not answer.

"LEWIS!" I knew he could hear me, he just wasn't listening. I kicked the garbage can he was sitting on and he finally looked up, the anger in his face matching mine. He knew who I was. I had chewed him out several times over the past few months, just like he had cussed and stormed at me, both in my house and in the street. Eventually we came to a compromise to stay on opposite ends of town, as the useless fighting wore both of us down.

His hands were blurry like Richard's, but dark spots could still be seen on his arms and face. He looked exactly like he did the day he hit my husband in the crosswalk.

I had looked it up; Lewis had no family. His roommates had pawned off his things, and his body had been cremated and placed in a cheap interment slot that no one visited except a distant cousin who didn't really know him.

"What?" he said angrily. "I thought we were staying the fuck away from each other."

"Watch your mouth," I spat. Lewis looked mad, but tired. He didn't bother getting off the garbage can, which was unusual, because one of his favorite things to do was get in my face and scream. There were a lot more things I wanted to say, things I already had said, but I bit them down. There was no time for it anymore.

"It's time to go. Come with us, and we can get you across now."

I didn't wait for him to respond, or to get up, or anything. I just left and walked back to the car, the car I'd been sitting in when I watched this stupid kid plow into my husband. He had passed out a few minutes later and died of an overdose. I don't remember it, but it was in the police report.

I slammed the door harder than I usually would have. Richard looked sadly at me, sandwiched between me and my mom. Darcy and Mom waited for me to do something, but all I could do was clench the wheel. Matilda clicked her tongue in the back seat. Silis whined.

Finally, Mom said, "We can't see him, Baby Daisy."

I clenched my fists so hard on the wheel that my joints hurt, and I reluctantly turned my head to the window. Lewis was standing there, arms crossed, looking in at us as if he was stuck out in the rain. I couldn't speak, but I nodded to the roof. Lewis put his foot on the hood and climbed up. I waited a few seconds, then sped off. I didn't look behind to see if he had fallen off.

The Light from A Thousand Suns

My cheek twitched, and I didn't look back when I got out of the car in the cemetery drive. I just marched off to where Janis, Mark, Tobias, and the kids were. When I remembered Richard and Silis, I turned back, but mother had already opened the door for Richard, and Silis was marching nobly next to Darcy.

"Over here!" called Janis, waving her arms from the large, grassy center of the cemetery. We hadn't picked the cemetery for its creepiness or its would-be connection to ghosts; we'd picked it because our town's cemetery was one of the nicest, most peaceful parks that you could go to in the middle of the night without being disturbed. There were old trees in the old section and a big grassy field in the center. The gravestones created side pastures surrounding the oval of grass. From a distance, the graves looked like spectators at a football game. In the center was a big monument with flags and statues of veterans and the past heroes of the community.

The moon was so bright we hardly needed a flashlight.

Darcy was playing with the iPad and looking up at the sky.

Richard floated next to me, looking up as well. I smiled. In the dark, I could pretend he was really there, standing next to me.

Darcy placed the iPad on the ground. A video of a sunset over the ocean was playing.

"I recorded it last week at the beach. Knew it would be handy." Janis skipped away from it and waited with Darcy and Tobias for something to happen.

Tobias asked the question first. "So, what are we waiting for?"

Mr. Grumpy was not bothering Tobias anymore. Instead, he was hunched over a placard in the rows of headstones. Tobias's complexion had greatly improved for it.

"The stars," said Grandma Lilly. "They are all suns, you know. Sometimes, spirits just need to be reminded that somewhere out there, there is a sun that is rising, setting, living, and dying."

"Then what?" asked Janis. But the question was answered for her when a ray of light appeared in the air above the iPad. It reminded me of sunlight coming through the kitchen window at Grandma Lilly's house. It grew until it was as tall as a standing mirror. Bugs and dust flecks glittered in it.

"Ooooh," said Matilda, reaching out her hand to the light. "It's beautiful."

"Sometimes it's easier to see the beauty of light when it's shrouded in darkness," said Grandma Lilly, and I wondered if she was aware of Matilda's observation. Matilda's eyes glowed like the light, and she walked into it. Before stepping in completely, she turned, blew me a kiss, then the light shone more brightly for an instant, and she was gone.

"One has passed," said Grandma Lilly. Everyone looked at me. I cleared my throat and looked sideways at Richard. "Matilda."

"How long is your sunset video?" asked Mom.

"About eight minutes," said Janis.

"Hmmm," said Mom, and looked at me with urgency. I glanced at the three spirits remaining. Lewis, I knew, didn't want to hear what I had to say, any more than I wanted to talk to him. And Mr. Grumpy...well, I don't think he cared that I existed.

I turned to my ghost of a husband.

"I need your help." It came out as a whisper, and I wasn't sure if he could hear me. But the grey figure next to me nodded and walked over to Mr. Grumpy at the memorial.

I followed.

Richard knelt next to Mr. Grumpy in the grass and gave a brief gesture of polite interest. Richard could do that, look at you like you could tell him anything. The part Mr. Grumpy would never know is that Richard could keep your words safe, too.

"I don't want to go," said Mr. Grumpy, his arms around his knees.

"Yeah," said Richard slowly. "Me neither."

"I spent all my time in that house," said Mr. Grumpy. "All the kids and grandkids. Julia...it happened so suddenly. I was getting some kettle corn for a movie, and I just sort of froze up. I don't even remember it hurting. It was just...done."

Richard nodded understandingly.

"I wasn't ready to be done. Emma's birthday was the next week. I was going to sit her on my knee and tell her about the time I went to Italy with Julia, long before we had kids. Long before we got married, for that matter. I saw a painting that looked just like Emma. The girl in the painting was a beautiful, regal queen. I wanted Emma to know she was a queen." He looked at Richard. "Do you think she knows she is a queen?"

Richard put his blurry hand on Mr. Grumpy's shoulder, and it seemed like an actual touch. Apparently, ghosts could feel each other. "Most good people tend to remember the best of us when we're gone."

Mr. Grumpy put his face in his hands and his shoulders shook, though I couldn't hear him crying, which was fine, because I was crying, and I could hear that just fine.

"What's your name?" asked Richard.

"Harrison," said Mr. Grumpy. "Nicola Harrison."

"Mr. Harrison, I think it's time to go."

Richard walked with Mr. Harrison to the sunlight mirror, and they spoke some more before he turned back to Tobias, mouthed "Sorry," and stepped into the light.

"Another gone," said Grandma Lilly.

"Mr. Harrison," I said.

Richard was already standing next to Lewis, who had his head down and his arms crossed.

"Hey," he said, not able to meet Richard's eyes. "Sorry, man."

Richard shrugged. "It's done."

"Yeah," said Lewis. He ran his hands through his short hair and fidgeted. "It's just, there's things I wanted to be, stuff I wanted to do. I never wanted it to end like this. I wanted to be someone."

Richard shrugged again. "Maybe you can be better next time around."

"Yeah," said Lewis. "There's some stuff I won't be doing again. You think I could be better? You think I'll remember this?"

"You remember what it feels like now," said Richard. "I don't see why you won't remember it later, when the time is right."

Lewis nodded a bunch of times and gave Richard a strained smile. He really was just a kid. Perhaps I had been too hard on him.

"Forgiveness can be easier in death," said Grandma Lilly.

Lewis stepped toward the light mirror, then hesitated briefly. Then he squared his shoulders and marched through, a bravery, I think, he wanted to carry with him wherever he went next.

Instead of telling everyone another had passed, Grandma Lilly flicked a tiny keychain light onto the iPad. It made the light mirror erupt, and it shone so brightly, everyone except Richard and I stepped back.

This was it. I had to say goodbye for the last time, and it was at that moment that I realized how much I didn't want to. Richard stood right in front of me, and with the light of the sun mirror behind him, he looked luminous, almost real. I knew there was little time, that I had to say goodbye, but there were only questions in my head, questions I had to have answered.

"Did I show you I loved you enough? Do you know you're my king? Did you feel like you did enough stuff? Do you know you meant everything?" I said, my throat clenching as I choked up.

Richard smiled his kind, welcoming smile, and he shook his head, ever so slightly. "Always."

I couldn't stifle the sobs, and it took everything I had not to reach out for him. He looked at me then, unsure, and he asked, "Do you hate me for dying?"

"I did at first," I said. "But it wasn't your fault. It was my fault."

"No, it wasn't," he said.

"We all die sometime," I said. "I'm glad—" I choked back enough tears to finish clearly. "I'm glad I had you when I did."

Richard smiled, and his face glowed. "I have to go now. Yvonne. You should go back."

"No, I don't want you to go," I said, even though a wind had arisen and it was so strong it stung my eyes and Silis was pulling on my sleeve. Even the faithful dog knew it was time to go, why didn't I? "It's not right. I can feel when things are right. This isn't right. You were not supposed to die!"

In that veil of wind and fire, Richard looked at me with his deep blue eyes. There was color in them again. He looked at me sweetly and rested his hands on my neck. It was all I could do to keep from throwing myself into his arms. Then my self-control failed, and I tried, but some magnetic force stopped me. Before I could completely break down, he said, "Look at me."

His voice wasn't dreamy and muddled like before, it was a beautiful, intoxicating symphony of tone, the music of his voice I loved; sweet clarity. I wanted desperately for him to stay. I wanted to tell him it was not fair, that all the romance novels were wrong. Paranormal romance was supposed to end with two lovers living together despite impossible odds. Why couldn't we have that? Why couldn't we have more time?

Those last two thoughts I spoke aloud without meaning to, and Richard's kind blue eyes regarded me patiently. Around me, the wind was blowing faster. Silis whined and retreated. My heart ached to go back to my dog, who was still alive, but I couldn't move, I couldn't leave.

"Pretend we are in the Fleetwood," he said, "and you're just getting ready to go to the movies."

"What?"

"Do it," he said, firmly but gently. I coughed back tears and did my best to breathe in the blistering wind. In my mind, I went back to the Fleetwood, the old chrome door handles that had some bubbles on the sides, the satisfying click as the door unlatched; I put my hand on the roof and the outside of the door, so my fingers would hit the barbed wire fence before the door did. I slid one foot in and shifted my weight; I forced myself to say it, stifling the terrible reality that it would be the last time.

"Hello, Richard."

"Open your eyes," Richard said. I hadn't even noticed my eyes were welded together fiercely. In my mind, I was looking at the dashboard, which was dusty and covered in nutshells that I hadn't swept away yet. I heard him next to me.

"Open your eyes."

In my mind, I looked up from the dashboard, but in reality, I forced my eyelids open. All that was in front of me was a white, twisting void.

Richard was gone.

"I'll see you in no time," I heard, and a warm finger lifted my bangs from my face. I could smell his hair, his unwashed jeans. I felt his soft breath even over the hot wind, but most of all, I felt his touch, a bolt of love that left my skin tingling all the way through my stomach and down through the earth. Suddenly, I felt connected, connected to the thing I don't like to explain but can only describe as love.

"Bye," we somehow whispered at the same time, and we shared the same sorrow, steadfast hope, and calm resolve.

I lingered, even though my mind told me not to. The light was spinning so fast.

"Yvonne!" screamed my mother, and her hand grabbed my arm before the portal could take me with it. I fell back into her arms as the shock of the blast sent us both sprawling into the grass.

A short time later, we were back at my house. Mark had made a fire pit in my backyard, and everyone was busying themselves with a late dinner. Grandma Lilly was sitting next to me on my low brick fence. The Fleetwood was parked in the driveway, and there was a pretty view of the neighbor's pond where the car used to be.

I told her everything. It all came out in a rush, but it felt good. It felt good to let go, and it felt good to sit under the cool starlight.

"Such is life. And it does go on, in the young ones and the things we leave behind. Is the pain of losing them not worth the delight it was having them?" said Grandma Lilly when I was finished.

"I don't know," I said. "This feels pretty bad."

She wrapped her thin arm around my shoulder and held it firmly. "Of course it does, but that is because you are in the throes of it, like you were once in the throes of love. Would you take it back?"

I didn't think I could answer.

Grandma Lilly kissed my cheek and walked carefully back to the fire pit. Stephanie met her halfway to help her.

"Hi, Yvonne," said Jasper, jumping up to sit next to me. I wiped the tears from my eyes and tried to smile at him.

"You're sad, huh?" he said.

"Yeah," I said.

"Is it something to do with Richard? I know it is his birthday today," he said.

"Oh yeah, it is," I said, remembering the birthdays I had been able to spend with Richard. That one time we saw a terrible movie but got ice cream afterward. The time we made a kennel for Silis, only to have it fall down and Silis travel with us in the car after all. The nights we spent afterward, where I would look at him and see a year older in his face, just like he probably saw a year older in mine.

"It's my birthday next week," Jasper offered. "I'll be twelve."

"Really?" I said, wiping my nose. "It feels like you just turned seven."

Jasper gave me a funny look. "Come on, Yvonne, that was like forever ago."

"Yeah, you are totally right," I said. "What do you want for your birthday?"

Jasper described in detail the various nuances of his favorite soon-to-be-released video games. When we came to a conclusion on the best game, we shook on it. Jasper laughed, then leaned over and wrapped his long arms around me and kissed my chin. "Be happy again, OK?"

I gave my nephew a hug right back and rubbed his arm. I couldn't help the tears in my eyes. "Damn right, buddy. Damn right. Uh...don't repeat that."

"I won't," he said cheerfully, then sprang off to attack Mark, who had procured a bag of marshmallows.

I heard the twanging of guitar strings and saw Darcy and Stephanie playing with Richard's guitars on the deck. Silis was lying on his side at their feet, perfectly content. Grandma Lilly, Mom, and Jasper were roasting marshmallows and hot dogs on sticks over the fire. Janis, Tobias, and Mark were sorting out the best place to put up the badminton net.

I pulled my Mt. Shasta blanket around me and looked up at the sky. Even with the light pollution, the stars were as bright as tiny suns. I felt empty beyond measure, and scared. It would be that way for a while, I knew. Only time could fill the void. But I was not alone. I had to realize, I was never alone, and my loves were never any closer or farther than the sky of suns, or the sound of guitar strings, or my dog's bark.

Jasper pulled a flaming marshmallow out of the fire and shouted, "Happy birthday, Richard!"

"Happy birthday, Richard!" everyone echoed in their own fashion. Silis howled once. It was the first time I had heard him do so.

The night was warm as I looked up at the stars, in wonder that they were all tiny suns, and that somewhere, a sun was rising, setting, and everything in between. A wisp of cloud floated across the moon, looking like a white cloud from the exhaust pipe of a familiar Cadillac. Somewhere Richard was driving on, across his Fleetwood skies.

"Magic doesn't exist," I reminded myself. "But we do, and that's pretty cool too."

Part II

Chime

For Kate, Supertwin and 24/7 answerer of obscure medical questions.

And special thanks to Dianne, who believed in Chime when I didn't.

Music is the voice for what the soul cannot say. What is a good-bye if not the echo of an empty heart?

- Meadowlark Book of Myths

Gold Dollar

Leandra Meadowlark

Beats.

Ba dump, ba dump, ba dump, says the heart.

Everywhere there is a cadence of sounds. Even the rolling tires of the bus progress in a rhythm; one is flatter than the rest.

Cathunk-thunk, cathunk-thunk.

The telltale crescendo of a bump; *cshink* as the chains rattle in the back of the bus. The road noise from passing cars approaching and fading.

Woooshooo.

Ba dump, cathunk-thunk, woooshooo.

Beats.

They are everywhere.

It was a lengthy trip over the mountains to Rockhouse, slowed because of ice. A young woman was listening to the sound of the bus in one ear and the intriguing melodies of a contemporary pianist through her headphones in the other. Every once in a while, she scribbled notes in a small notebook.

Leandra Meadowlark's dark hair fell from under her hood as she leaned forward to write down her thoughts quickly. Sometimes the rhythms slipped away as another rhythm emerged. The good ones always came back to her eventually, but she liked to read the beats later. She could remember things from the beats, as if they were a diary.

Sound and smell hold the most memories, Leandra had written in her master's thesis.

Beats and rhythms were Leandra's comfort, until a rhythm sounded too familiar.

The hurried scraping of jeans, *schrich schrich schrich,* someone running fast.

Leandra sat up quickly as a small boy ran past her from the bathroom to the front of the bus. The sound had startled her.

The boy sat back down with his mother in the front. Leandra rubbed her eyes and pulled her hood back to swipe her hair away from her eyes. She had left in such a hurry that she had forgotten the short-brimmed cap that usually kept it under control.

Leandra returned her attention to the rhythms of the bus and the cadence of road noise and chains.

Citunk a tunk-tunk, ca, citunk a tunk-tunk.

But the beat was off. Leandra's heart was pounding just a little too fast. She took a deep breath, put her notebook back in her pack, and scanned through her music to find something distracting.

It was already going to be a hard day. The past had no room to haunt her today.

She was startled a second time when she heard disheartened crying.

Leandra looked up at the only other passengers on the bus, the woman and two children at the front. The mother had explained to the bus driver, in a tired but optimistic voice, that their clutch had given out at the end of their vacation. They had decided to take the bus home instead of waiting for the time-consuming repair.

It was 1:00 a.m., and the bus was loud and bright. The kids were tired and wanted to sleep, but they couldn't in such an uncomfortable and unfamiliar place. There were many hours still to go.

Leandra watched the young girl cry, waking her mother. She sobbed that she wanted to go back and stay with Grandpa Peter; it had been so much fun. Going home meant going back to school, homework, and school lunches.

The mother tiredly said, "Shhh, try to sleep." But the girl would not stop crying softly.

Most would have dismissed the sound of crying or turned up the volume on their headphones. Leandra could not ignore it.

She wrapped her headphone cord around her phone and zipped it away safely in her backpack. She left her pack in the far seat by the window because she was sure it would be safe.

Though the heaters hissed out stale air, sounding to Leandra eerily like a chanting chorus, it was chilly. The windows had fogged and frozen from the inside.

Leandra walked to the front of the bus, her head almost scraping the ceiling. She sat down in the seat opposite the crying girl, who looked at her self-consciously.

Leandra smiled and held up her hands. "Pick a hand."

The girl looked up inquisitively at her mother. Her mother nodded politely.

The young girl pointed to one of Leandra's hands. Leandra waved that hand, closed her fingers briefly into a fist, and then opened her hand. Two shiny gold dollars sat side by side like eyes. The girl's own eyes widened with a tentative curiosity.

Leandra began to flip the coins across her knuckles, over both hands, and through her fingers in a dizzying display of coin and finger acrobatics. The young girl looked amazed, and her brother woke up to watch as well.

Leandra ended the show by flicking the two coins high in the air and catching them in unison in the palm of her hand. She then held out the coins for the children to take, bowing her head slightly with the finale. They took the shiny gold dollars from her hand with glee.

"You want me to show you how?" Leandra asked.

They nodded enthusiastically. Their mother beamed with gratitude. It only took about twenty minutes of teaching, then Leandra went back to her seat. The children practiced studiously with their coins, sometimes retrieving them from off the floor, sometimes losing them in the folds of their coats, but always bringing them back to their palms with wonder. It was enough to fill the emptiness and relieve the boredom of the bus ride. Eventually, the children fell asleep against their mother, holding the coins safely in their hands, no doubt dreaming of magic.

Only then did Leandra go back to her rhythms in the sounds of the bus. There was a long ride to go, and she wished something as simple as coin tricks could make her go to sleep.

She dismissed the memories attached to the sound of scraping jeans.

Not today...not today.

She longed to sleep, but sleeping meant dreams, and there would be no comforting dreams for her right then. So she listened to the sounds of the bus, nodding her head and keeping the beat.

Ca-thunk thunk, woooshooo.

It's only a memory.

Ca-thunk thunk, cshink.

Road Trip

Yvonne Meadowlark Rainier

I shivered as I felt my head touch a spider web. I flipped my hand through my hair just in case a spider had fallen into it. My job is to evict ghosts from houses for sale, but that doesn't mean I enjoy the creepy things that go with it.

"You all right, Yva?" called my sister, Janis, from below. My little nephew, Timmy, was strapped into a baby carrier across her chest. Timmy added some baby garble to her inquiry.

"Yeah," I said grumpily. I was the obvious candidate to go into the attic, because I didn't have an infant strapped to my chest, and I was also the only one of us who could see ghosts.

"See her?" Janis called.

I shivered from the spider webs and the cold and shined my flashlight around the tiny attic. Along with a few dozen more spider webs, I spotted the faint grey outline of Mildred Addicus's ghost leaning over the floorboards.

"Hi Ms. Addicus," I said and waved.

Ms. Addicus didn't look up from the spot on the floor.

"Anything?" asked Janis from the brightly lit and spider-free hallway below.

"No," I said, disheartened. "Mildred?" I tried.

The ghost of Mildred Addicus looked up curiously. "Have you seen my flowerpots?" she said softly.

"Oh," I said. "Yeah, they are outside. Do you want to come see them?"

"Oh…" Mildred trailed off. "Oh…no…I'm sure I left them up here somewhere."

"No, no no no," I said, scampering across the rickety floor, ducking the webs as much as I could. I was afraid that she would disappear again, and Janis and I were already working overtime. "Let's try this, OK? Can I show you something?" I got to the attic window, which was awkward because I had to walk through her to do it, and opened the shutters. I pointed down at the garden. "See? There they are."

"Oh," said Mildred happily, "that's where I left them." Mildred's grey ghost floated to the window to serenely inspect her garden. Janis and I had spent the afternoon clearing it of snow and placing fake flowers from the dollar store around the paths. Ghosts like to see things they love flourish, and it's a good way to get them to cross.

I watched in anticipation as Mildred's grey eyes slowly looked up to the sun setting through the trees. Her face softened with wonder, and her ghost evaporated and disappeared like smoke.

"Phew," I sighed with relief. "Bye, Mildred," I said, closing the shutters and maneuvering as best I could out of the small attic.

"Did she go?" asked Janis, playing with Timmy's feet.

"Yep," I said, closing the attic door. I shook off all the spider webs and went to wash my hands. "Text Mom and let her know."

"OK, I'll meet you at the car," said Janis, opening her phone. Her face scrunched up as she read a waiting text. "Ah, Mark isn't getting off until eleven."

"Aw," I said, shaking my hands dry because I didn't want to mess up Darcy's expertly folded display towels. "You can always come hang out at my house, eat burritos, and binge watch Model with me and Silis."

Janis's face brightened to a shade of happy that complemented her orange glasses. "Excellent!"

The plan was wonderful, but it didn't last long.

I had emerged from a delightful shower and was in my comfy I-just-did-a-hard-day's-work pajamas. Timmy was bouncing around in a nest of couch cushions and pillows with his bottle and blanket. My phone rang just as Janis and I got comfortable with our bag of burritos and large cups of soda. The call was from Grandma Lilly, so I answered immediately.

"I just Saw something, Baby Daisy," Grandma Lilly said without preamble.

I held the phone at a distance while trying to keep my face away from my baby nephew's prying hands. "Hang on, Tim. What's up, Gram?"

"Your mother's on her way to your house," said Grandma Lilly. "You and Silis are going with her to Rockhouse. Be sure to bring your jacket."

What do you say to Grandma Lilly but "OK"?

"What's Gram up to?" Janis asked, taking baby Timmy from my arms as I crossed to the bedroom. I emerged with an old duffel bag and threw some clean clothes into it from a basket on the couch.

"She Saw me go with Mom to Rockhouse." I got a ziplock bag from the kitchen and filled it with dog food. Silis sniffed at it excitedly. "No, goob, you don't get two dinners."

"Aw, no Model?" said Janis with a mouthful of steak burrito.

"No, but feel free to stay. What time is Mark getting off, again?"

"Eleven," said Janis, then she grimaced at the time on her cellphone. "You're going to be driving all night."

Silis turned his sleek Doberman ears attentively to the front door as Mom's car rolled into the gravel driveway.

"You want to go see Grandma?" Janis said in a singsong voice. Timmy smiled toothlessly and blew a raspberry. He did that when he was excited. It was both cute and gross.

Janis and Timmy went outside to see Mom as I packed hastily. I begrudgingly changed out of my comfy pajamas and found some warm clothes that would be comfortable to drive in. When I emerged from the bedroom, Silis looked up guiltily, his face in the bag of burritos.

"Oh, you dirty dog."

"So, what are we doing?" I asked Mom in the driveway as I ate the last remaining burrito. Silis was sitting happily in the back seat of my Trooper.

Mom sighed regally. "Do you remember the Harrow fiasco?" she said finally.

Janis and I both grimaced.

"You mean Uncle Gerald's crazy wife and that cult they had going on a few years ago?" I said.

"Gerald's wife's sister's cult, but yes," said Mom, putting her designer overnight bag in the back of the Trooper next to mine.

Janis gave me a look of pity laced with "better you than me." My sisters and I did our best to stay away from that part of the family.

"So we have to deal with them?" I asked dryly.

"They are reading Antigone's will," said Mom, pulling out her tablet to review her meticulously kept schedule.

"Finally?" said Janis. Mom nodded.

"Good grief," I said, wadding up my burrito wrapper and throwing it at the garbage can. It missed. "How am I involved in this?"

"Grandma said she Saw you there," said Mom, and that was it.

"OK," I said skeptically. "Did either one of you See me?" Mom and Janis could both See bits of the future sometimes. My older sister Darcy and I were normal—at least, I had been until about a year ago, when my husband died and I began to see ghosts all the time.

"No, dear," said Mom, "but I wouldn't doubt what your grandmother Saw."

Janis shrugged. "I haven't Seen much since Timmy was born."

"Okey dokey then," I said.

We said good-bye and got settled in the car. Just as we were leaving the driveway, I hit the brakes.

"Wait," I said to a perplexed mother and an alert dog. "I forgot my jacket."

"What happened to the food?" Janis asked as I came through the door.

"Dog."

A night's worth of driving later, we were just entering the Rockhouse city limits.

It would have been easier to drive through the night if I could have listened to my music really loud over the recently installed sound system in my Trooper, but Mom was with me, and she did not share my taste for alternative rock. We both loved certain classical music, but I would have fallen asleep listening to Bach. Mom was reading her book. If she noticed the foul cloud of pungent dog gas that crept into the front seat like a deadly wave of mustard gas, she kept it to herself. The Doberman in question was napping happily in the back, completely oblivious to the turbulent death cloud he had just created.

I would not be eating burritos for a long while.

I tapped my fingers on the steering wheel, thinking.

"Hey, Mom," I said after a while, "do you think there's something up with the ghosts not crossing?"

"Hm?" she said, placing her finger on the place she'd left off in her book. She had slept most of the night but still had already read through one paperback. Silis was stretched out in the back seat, waking up reluctantly. He yawned loudly.

"Lately it's been weird that the ghosts aren't crossing. You know, like Richard and the others last summer, and all the others we've been seeing recently. I wonder why?"

"Hard to tell, Baby Daisy," said Mom, placing her fancy beaded bookmark in her paperback. "Sometimes things just go in phases, like the moon."

"Hm." I saw a bright neon sign for 24-hour coffee. "Think we can make them wait a few more minutes?"

"Yes, please," she said tartly.

"Done." I made a bit of a risky turn into the drive-through to beat a car full of commuters and turned the engine off so the attendant could hear our order.

A Chime was recorded on the payroll of a small Montana coal mine in 1917. His salary was an extra dollar a season more than the rest. If a miner died in the tunnels, the Chime would sing into the maze before anyone returned to work. The owners and workers alike did not care that the echo could cause a cave-in, or that the delay slowed production. The Chime, to them, was absolutely necessary, especially if nobody could retrieve the body to be brought to the tiny cemetery on the hill.

They wanted to know that the tunnels did not harbor the souls of angry ghosts. What's more, the Chime kept the living in a state of higher morality. "A miner spends his days far deeper than a grave," one of the miners told me. "Can't do to keep his mind like he's in one."

The mine was abandoned when the Chime died. Who would Chime for him?

- Meadowlark Book of Myths

BEATRICE

Leandra Meadowlark, City of Rockhouse

"Don't let this get in the way of what you got to do today, Leandra," said Beatrice curtly, breaking the awkward silence. "You gonna let them see you cry?"

"No," I said defensively. "Of course not."

Beatrice nodded in her decisive way, reminiscent of her years spent in the navy, and it was both curt and approving. Her voice bit like a shark, authoritative and true. "I thought you'd say that."

Beatrice was easy to talk to because she was just as stubborn as I was. She was a sixty-four-year-old navy veteran who never let her short stature give any impression that she was less than navy stock. She had been all but forced to retire at age fifty-four and begrudgingly took to the boring life of being the landlady of the house she had inherited from her parents.

Beatrice lived upstairs, Dad and I lived downstairs. She was our landlady, but she also watched me when Dad was working, which was a lot.

She never put up with any shit from teenage me, and eventually I learned how to not put up with any shit from her. Eight years I had known her, and today would be the last.

Beatrice was dead. The apparition of Beatrice sitting next to me was her ghost.

We sat in the backyard of the property on the old metal lawn furniture. The sun wasn't up yet, but the sky was dusty with predawn light. It had been colder on the bus ride in the mountains, but it was still chilly for November.

I pulled an old harmonica out of my coat pocket. Beatrice had given me the coat: sturdy canvas or something like it, tailored for a woman, lots of pockets, insulated, and not pink. I don't know where she found it, but it was one of the best gifts I had ever gotten: not flashy, clean looking, and functional, all traits that seemed to be the opposite of what people make women's clothes for. I had patched the coat several times, nicely. Not even my old social worker would have argued about how good it looked. I don't carry much with me, but I keep what I have nice.

Beatrice's ghost smiled at the old harmonica dancing between my fingers. Even in the bite of the cold November morning, the harmonica was warm from my pocket. I was just getting off work from a night shift at the campus library when I learned

Beatrice was dead. I left a message for my boss at the college; I would be gone for the rest of the semester. I packed up my things, which all fit in one bag, and rode my longboard to the only open bus station.

I hadn't slept much that night, and I didn't expect to sleep much for a while.

There wasn't much left of Beatrice's ghost, which said a lot about her character. Ghosts are lost people, usually, and Beatrice was never lost. She had chosen to stay, and I suspected she had decided to stick around for me.

The backyard was still in shadow, which made it easier to pretend that Beatrice was sitting, solid and alive, next to me, though I knew unequivocally that she wasn't.

I always knew she would stay around and make me do the Chime for her. She knew it's what I needed to let her go.

"Come on, kid," Beatrice's ghost said, with the strange, hollow, gargled sound that ghosts talk with. "Give me a good Chime. I got places to go."

I could already tell there wasn't much of Beatrice left. She didn't breathe. Beatrice moved a certain way when she breathed, and she wasn't doing it now. I tried not to look at her. I learned a long time ago that looking just makes the job harder.

"You want me to tell Martin anything?" I asked, raising the harmonica to my lips.

"Yogi?" Beatrice nodded knowingly about her brother Martin, whom she always called Yogi. "Tell him to move back to Texas and get his motorcycle back."

Martin sat at the kitchen table in silence, watching Leandra sitting in one of the old lawn chairs on the back porch. He hadn't seen Leandra since she had gone off to college a few years before. She had been back a few times, of course, but Martin's job as a truck driver had an unpredictable schedule at best. His semi was parked outside. No trailer was hooked up at the moment.

Martin and Leandra left things for each other at Beatrice's house, mostly albums, though Martin usually left an iTunes gift card with some obscure band scribbled on a sticky note. Martin didn't know how to use them, but Leandra liked to keep all her possessions on her tablet and computer.

Leandra left Martin CDs that he listened to on his long truck drives, and they would text each other about the bands. Some were good, some sucked. Leandra confessed to him once that she just really loved the album covers, but that the ones with good album covers usually had terrible music, and vice versa.

There was a small closet where Beatrice had put some of the things from Leandra's younger days that Gerald had found, but she never looked at them.

They were things Leandra wanted to forget.

Martin hadn't taken any contracts since Beatrice's health had taken a turn for the worse a few months before.

Beatrice had been adamant that Martin not alert Leandra to her declining health. "She knows how it's going to go," Beatrice had said, still fierce, though the disease had all but reduced her to a shadow of her former self. "She's seen enough. She knows what the end is for me. Let her come when she comes."

Martin had honored this, reluctantly. It had been a hard few weeks, and he had barely slept, watching over his sister. Beatrice had told him this was the hardest part, this waiting game. "Don't get lost over me, Yogi," she had said in a gravelly voice.

After Beatrice had passed, Martin had gotten out his worn-out cellphone and texted Leandra. She had responded so quickly that Martin had been startled by the text ringtone.

On my way. Bringing the Chime.

The coroner had already come to take Beatrice's body the previous night. Yogi had slept a bit, but not much. He was waiting for Leandra and

Gerald, and then he'd find something else to do, some other place to go.

Martin tapped the table absently as he watched the sun begin to rise over the fields behind the house. Leandra was tapping her harmonica and saying things he could not quite hear through the glass. The chair next to her was empty, but Martin knew the ghost of his sister must have been sitting there.

Beatrice understood Leandra's past better than most. She was there when Leandra's dad, Gerald, was up for days researching laws and finding the right lawyers, and when he'd get frustrated and break something, she would grab a bottle of bourbon and two glasses and pull him out into the yard to talk with her over a drink. Beatrice was there when Leandra came to live with him after the events at Winter Hill. She watched the girl read books on the roof and throw rocks at passing cars.

As a Chime, Gerald traveled a lot, and Leandra was left with Beatrice. Both of them were headstrong, with wills of iron. Martin remembered times when he'd come to visit, late at night after a long job, and ask where Leandra was. Beatrice would wave her hand toward the open fields behind the house, where several rocky hills dotted the distance. "Out there somewhere."

"Should I go look for her?" he would ask.

"Nah," Beatrice would say. "She's right there."

Leandra would come back hours later, covered in dust and sweat, as if she had crawled out of a cave, and head straight for the kitchen. She would have two bowls of cereal eaten before she even said hello.

Martin was lifted from his memories when Leandra started to play the harmonica, long, echoing notes that demanded attention. The tune was a long, calm melody that was reminiscent of his childhood.

He could almost hear the words of the Simon and Garfunkel song, like Beatrice used to sing along with on the radio.

Martin fiddled with the saltshaker to distract himself from his sudden tears.

I put everything I had into that song for Beatrice.

I remembered the nights I'd run for miles through the fields behind the house to the hills. They were always farther away than they looked. They were far back into the desert. No one ever went out there. I'd climb the hills and look back on the world I had run from. No matter how far I ran, Beatrice left the porch light on for me. I always could see where to go back to.

She understood that I needed to run. I never knew where or for how long or why, but I would get an itch and get nervous, and I would run out into the fields as if I was running for my life. I'd stop miles later, covered in grass and dirt. Sometimes it was cold, and sometimes it was dark. Sometimes I got sunburned. One time I was sick and had to lie down in the dirt and wild grass for a few hours before I could get back to the house.

Beatrice never questioned it. She just left the back porch light on and kept the cupboards stocked with food for when I got back.

She lived longer than any of the doctors predicted, long enough to see me through a diploma and off to college a few hours away. We didn't talk about her illness. The end was something we both knew was coming. Then, one day, she told me her favorite song, and I remember she said it with a finality that was more than a casual remark.

She was telling me what she wanted for her Chime, and she was looking at my harmonica and me as if she expected something.

She never lied about her illness. The first day we met, Beatrice pulled me aside and told me straight out, "Kid, I'm going to die. I'm taking medicines and prescriptions that would kill a lesser human, and that's the way it is. One day soon, I won't be here anymore."

I was fourteen. I had a cast on my arm, a sling that rubbed painfully on my neck, and what the adults were telling me was a black eye. I don't remember getting the black eye.

Beatrice was the first adult besides Dad who didn't treat me like a skittish pet. The social workers, lawyers, and officers talked to me like you'd talk to a stray dog; their voices high-pitched and full of self-righteous concern. I hated it. I'd broken my wrist, not my fucking eardrums.

"OK," I had said with a calmness that had concerned the social workers who'd insisted they inspect Beatrice's house with me. I just wanted them to go away. Beatrice nodded and poured me a bowl of cereal. I ate the whole thing and ignored the overly forced optimism of the social workers who tried to get me to talk about how I felt about staying with my father and his landlady, Beatrice.

I had learned some good swear words from books, and I used them.

Beatrice laughed and shooed the social workers away. She left the box of cereal and milk on the kitchen counter and went to watch TV.

I remember the buzz of the little TV as she watched nothing in particular. She sorted through a stack of paperback books as I ate bowl after bowl of cereal.

Beatrice left me alone, and it was such a relief.

We didn't need to say much, ever. We fought, sure, but that was just blowing off steam. We both had a lot of steam. It worked out.

Today I wasn't running through the fields. Today I was doing my job and Chiming for her. Dad taught me how to Chime, and when I got out of Winter Hill, I studied it painstakingly. Eight years on, I'm really good at it.

I blew cold November air through the reeds of the harmonica and twitched my hand to create vibrato. I had been practicing the song since the day Beatrice had told me it was her favorite.

Ghosts hear music, and it helps them cross to whatever's next. That's what the Chime is for.

Yeah, it's really just me playing a harmonica loudly to a ghost that no one else can see, but a real Chime gives a ghost direction.

Dad used to say the Chime is like the Pied Piper leading the rats away from the city with his flute, only we do it for ghosts. The Chime just reminds them that they have somewhere to be, like an alarm clock.

It's an honor march, and I think it's beautiful.

The harmonica belonged to my grandfather, then my dad, then me. Any instrument or sound will do for a Chime, but this one is mine.

I close my eyes when I play. I never know if the Chime works until it is over, and the last note is gone.

The ghost of Beatrice watched Leandra play with self-satisfied pride. She knew it would help Leandra to do the Chime. Leandra had grown into a very capable young woman, but Beatrice saw the wounds still fresh underneath the surface.

Beatrice had the good fortune to have seen the real Leandra on rare occasions: the gem inside the battered skin, the beautiful woman behind the atrocities she should have never seen, the responsibilities she should have never had to carry.

Beatrice understood.

The harmonica's tune filled the air, and Beatrice felt a spark of something warm she had not felt since she was alive. A glint of light caught Beatrice's eye, and she turned to the sun, now rising brilliantly over the house. It glowed over the fields and looked so welcoming, so happy to see her.

"Oh," she said, and stood up with no pain. "There you are."

Something distracted her. She turned from the sun. Another ghost stood in the shadows. She wore a cardigan and long skirt. Her hair was long and curled at the ends. She smiled and waved at Beatrice.

"Hmm," said Beatrice with concern. She looked back momentarily at Leandra playing the harmonica. "I'm sorry, girl, but I'm afraid it's not done yet," she said quietly.

I finished on one long, low note, and I let the little reeds inside the harmonica resonate to silence before I opened my eyes and looked over at the chair next to me.

Beatrice was gone.

Martin scratched his head when I opened the screen door. Bits of tissue were stuck in his mustache and beard. I hadn't watched much of the Yogi cartoon, but I imagined that they had based the bear off him, though the show was older than he was. I smiled at him encouragingly, and he nodded.

Now that the Chime for Beatrice was over, there was another matter I needed to deal with. Today was a day I had intended to be as far from Rockhouse as possible.

"Your dad called me. He's going to meet us at the lawyer's office," said Martin.

I nodded, shouldered my bag, and grabbed my longboard. There were going to be people at the lawyer's office whom I had never intended to see again. But Beatrice's death had put me in town, and some things are just too coincidental to ignore as fate.

It's not as if I wasn't invited. It was my mother's will they were going to read, after all.

Martin's old Chevy truck smelled familiar and nostalgic as I slid in. As we waited for the truck to warm up, I told him what Beatrice had said.

"Texas, huh?" Martin said. "Well, I do miss my motorcycle."

Vampires

Leandra Meadowlark

"Who's here?" I asked in the parking lot of an auto shop a few blocks away from the lawyer's office. The parking lot was surrounded by trees, and it was unlikely anyone would see us there. Well, see me there. It was also cold, so no one was likely to bother us.

"Juliet for sure," said my dad, Gerald, handing me a burger.

"No lawyer?" asked Martin, drinking iced tea out of his giant soda cup.

"No," said Dad, eating a few of his french fries quickly. He had eaten his burger by the time we'd gotten there.

Dad looked about the same as the last time I'd seen him: handsome, dark, and too young for the troubled lines permanently etched into his face. We were often told how much we resembled one another. I always wondered if it was because I was tall like he was or if we shared the same look.

We'd decided it would be best to meet up and eat before the meeting. None of us expected anything really bad to happen, but we also didn't expect everything to go smoothly. Since it was my fault that everything had gone south at Winter Hill, we all wanted to be careful.

"What's going to happen, exactly?" I asked, taking a huge bite of my burger.

"Well," said Dad, flicking salt off his fingers and leaning on the bumper of his old Ford Bronco. "The lawyer is going to read what they've found to be her final will. They will make sure the items are delegated out correctly, and we'll leave."

"That's it?" I said.

"Yep," said Dad.

"Should go smoothly?" I said.

"Should," said Dad.

"Who else is going to be there?" asked Martin, who looked over automatically at the semi-truck driving by, inspecting it for things only semi-truck drivers inspect other semis for.

"Bjorn and Lester, maybe. There also might be representatives of the press."

I groaned and sipped my fountain drink special: an intuitive mixture of whatever the soda fountain had to offer.

"I don't think they'll give you any trouble," said Dad, meaning he would see to it that they wouldn't give me any trouble.

Winter Hill was old news to everyone except those who were involved in it. The media had a field day for the first few years afterward, but then some new crisis would happen and the masses would move on to obsessing over the next big bout of national trauma. People only cared about you as long as you were interesting or newsworthy.

Martin interrupted my thoughts. "Is Olivia coming?"

"Uh huh," said Dad, looking at his phone. "Yvonne too. They stopped at the coffee joint on Main and are heading to the office. Do you remember them?" he asked me.

"Wow," I said, swirling the remaining ice in my soda cup, recalling my brief encounter with my cousins on Dad's side. They were older than I was, but familiar in a funny way, as if they all had something about them that reminded me of Dad. "That was forever ago."

"Was it the family reunion?" said Dad. "What was that, fifteen years ago?"

"Yeah," I said. "Long time."

Yvonne Meadowlark Rainier

"Do you remember that family reunion like, fifteen years ago?" I said to Mom, taking long glugs of the mocha frappe-fancy-something I'd ordered on impulse. After ordering drinks, we'd decided to go in and get some food. I usually don't drink foo-foo coffee, but it seemed like an occasion that warranted caffeine, sugar, and fancy breakfast sandwiches. The two sausage breakfast muffins I had already consumed were doing a moderately satisfying job of combating the stimulants.

"Yes," said Mom, sipping her caramel Americano with grace. Somehow her outfit exquisitely matched the coffee cup, and I wondered if she'd planned it. "That was the last time I saw Leandra and Tori. Do you remember them?"

"Yeah," I said, balancing my drink on the roof as I unlocked the door with the key. My car was old enough that it did not have automatic locks. "Is Tori Juliet's daughter? Leandra and Tori were inseparable at that reunion."

"Yes," said Mom, patiently waiting for me to unlock her door. Silis sniffed her scone through the open window. Mom broke off a piece and gave it to him after I got my drink safely settled and leaned over to unlatch the door. "We should hurry."

"Spoiled dog," I said, scratching Silis's chin. Mom closed the door and sipped her coffee as I turned on the GPS to find the lawyer's office. "Why?"

Mom scrolled through her text messages. "Leandra is going to be there."

"Really? Whoa," I said, clicking the GPS into place on the window holder. "I thought Juliet was going to be there too?"

"She is," said Mom pensively.

"Wow." Suddenly I was even more thankful for the mocha-frappa-something; I wanted to be awake for this. "Uncle Gerald is going to be there too, right?"

"Yes," said Mom.

I slurped the last of my frappe and wished I had gotten a larger one. "I know we have weird lives because of the ghosts and Seeings and stuff, but really, Antigone's sister Juliet ran a cult. She's like, almost kind of related to us. It just seems so weird and gross. What would she be?"

"She's your uncle's wife's sister," said Mom. "A distant relation."

"Well, she can stay over there," I said, flinging crumbs out the window before turning on the engine to get the heater going.

"Hm," Mom huffed in agreement. She pulled out her book, sifted through a few more pages and scowled, then put the book back in her bag. She pulled out another with a much different cover than the usual supernatural romance variety.

I chuckled at the shirtless man with the telescope and something with "Fever" in the title. "Last one was no good, huh?"

"Terrible," she said tartly, "and I'm not in the mood for vampires."

Leandra Meadowlark

I found a book once with vampires who sparkled and drove Volvos. It was very worn out, because several other members of the cult liked to read it. I should have taken that as a clue to how terrible it would be. Suffice it to say, I didn't get very far, and I ended up using it to set fire to the garden shed.

I don't think vampires drink blood and shrink away from the sun and personal relationships. I think the opposite is true; vampires love relationships. They love to give you something you want so they can use it against you. Vampires are manipulative and suck the life out of you. Sometimes it's a worse feeling than getting your blood drawn.

Psychologists call them narcissists. They suck away your happiness and ruin your life. I hate narcissists. It's easy to be an asshole; it's harder to be a decent human being, which requires a certain level of self-sufficiency and compassion. All the "vampires" I've ever met steal the lives of everyone around them.

The cult members of Winter Hill were vampires, led by my Aunt Juliet. People gave them money, supported them, bought their rhetoric, and tried to impress them, believing they were all-powerful beings like the vampires in the bad vampire novel.

They didn't realize that they were monsters.

There are two ways to survive being stuck with vampires: become a vampire or stay away from them. In fiction, the best way is to kill them, but I don't think that's the right thing in real life.

The simple truth is that vampires are monsters; the evil kind.

I thought about this as I drove with Dad to the lawyer's office. I was relieved to see only a few cars in the parking lot. I'd been worried that it would be a giant media shitstorm like it had been after the incident. The media had been so crazy that I'd had to wait for the following year to start school again.

Dad put me in public school briefly once. I think the first thing that went wrong was that the teachers were all too nice to me. Then the other girls started asking me stupid questions, like "Are you OK?" and "Was Lester as cool in person as he was on Twitter?" But mostly it was the gym. They expected me to get undressed in front of a bunch of other girls and touch other people in gym class. I said no and left. They were especially displeased when they found out I was ditching gym to play on the drum set in the band room. The only one who didn't mind was the band teacher, who said I kept better time than most of his drummers.

They threatened to suspend me.

I shrugged and said, "OK."

That seemed to piss them off.

I compromised by arriving to gym class fifteen minutes late. I showed up for the sit-ups and running, and dribbled the basketball around, but I refused to get undressed in the locker room. The gym teachers seemed really confused when I continued to tell them no.

By the end of the first week, all the kids were pointing me out and sniggering. I went to the principal's office with one of the deans, and Dad was there. They talked about some weird curriculum I didn't understand, and that was the end of public school.

Dad bought a book on the curriculum and homeschooled me. Which really meant that Beatrice showed me what I needed to learn, then took me to the library and said, "Figure it out."

I read a lot. I took some tests at various schools with some other homeschooled kids. I almost didn't pass the first few because I kept asking questions and making comments during the tests, mostly along the lines of "This is stupid, why did this question get worded this way?" and "I don't do math like this. You want me to do this weird-ass way of math, and I do it this way and still get the correct answer, only quicker."

Also, I had conversations like this: "Don't swear in the classroom!" "Why the fuck not?"

There were some snags, but I graduated with honors.

I worked hard on college scholarship essays, though most of the scholarships were practically shoved into my hands at the mention of Winter Hill. I nodded politely to all the sympathetic adults, but secretly knew they had no idea what they were talking about.

In truth, I didn't need to finish out this semester of college. I had all the classes I needed for my degree, but I decided to take on a few more to get another minor. I could decide later if I wanted to bother finishing it or not.

I don't define my life by Winter Hill. A lot has happened in the eight years since then, but like what happened with the sound of scraping jeans, the memories come back.

I am not who I was, I remind myself. I am not who I was. The vampires cannot hurt us now.

Dad and I surveyed the parking lot in silence as we pulled up to the lawyer's office. We were both watching and waiting for something to happen.

"You can leave your backpack in here," he said, pointing to an old metal ammunition container he'd gotten at the army surplus store. I leaned over awkwardly and stowed my bag in it. We got out and walked slowly to the front door.

I listened to each of our steps, following the cadence. I found the rhythm and counted on it to get us from the car to the door. The morning glare was bright, but the air was cold.

A silver sports car was sitting across the lot, and I recognized who was standing by the vehicle.

"Bjorn and Lester," said Dad.

We reached the door at the same time. My cousins were tall, and dark like me. Bjorn was my age. He had dark circles under his eyes and a strained expression. He was much thinner than I remembered. Lester was a few years older than us. His looks had made him the poster child for the cult, but he had aged poorly in eight years. His face was too sharp, his eyes too cold. The years had not been kind to them.

I had grown. I could look them in the eyes now.

"Uncle Gerald," said Lester slyly.

"Boys," said Gerald, opening the glass door and gesturing for them to go in. They hesitated, and Lester looked as if he might have said something, but then he went through without a word. Bjorn gave me a strange look before entering. We waited at the door until they went past the receptionist and into the lawyer's office.

I gasped and had to take a few deep breaths, grabbing my knees to prevent myself from falling over. At last, I straightened and shook out my wrists. Dad stood tensely at the door, watching the parking lot and the building for anyone approaching.

"Ready?" he said. He knew I wouldn't go wait in the car.

"Yeah," I said curtly.

"I'm right behind you."

"I know."

What Remains, Whose Hands

Yvonne Meadowlark Rainier

"Stay here, crazy dog," I said to Silis as I cracked the windows for him. He whined and sniffed the sausage sandwich wrapper I shoved into my coat. "No, goob-dog, this isn't for you."

"Still has the Bronco," Mom said, and chuckled at the old Bronco we parked near.

"Whose is it?" I asked as we got out.

"Gerald's." Mom's shoes clicked melodically across the cold pavement. "He bought it when he graduated."

The receptionist smiled up at us as the glass door closed behind us. "Mrs. Meadowlark and Mrs. Rainier?"

She smiled and pointed down to a door. I opened it and did not expect what I saw.

I saw a ghost.

She was grey, with a curly bob of hair reminiscent of the 1940s. She wore a cardigan, and a poodle skirt as well. She turned around when I opened the door and looked at us. She smiled at me, put her grey finger to her mouth, and said, "Shh."

Then she skated out the door on four-wheeled, strap-on roller skates.

I pretended I had to sneeze, because the bewilderment on my face was awkwardly apparent. Mom stepped into the office and greeted her brother Gerald warmly. He stood in the back of the room with a young woman I didn't recognize until she looked up at us. Gerald and Leandra have the same eyes, honey yellow and piercing, like a hawk's. It used to really creep me out until Janis pointed out that mine are somewhat similar.

"Hey!" I said, and gave Gerald a hug. He grinned like a teenager, with dimples in his cheeks. It was adorable, and I told him so.

"Oh," he said, and laughed nervously. I punched him on the arm affectionately. I turned to Leandra and held out my hand, as she didn't look like a person who wanted to be hugged. "Hey, I'm Yvonne. It's been a few million years."

Leandra smirked, amused. She shook my hand somewhat tentatively, but her handshake was firm. "Yeah, it has," she said.

"Here, ladies," said one of the Harrows, the older one, Lester, I thought. He pulled an empty chair back and winked at me.

"I'm good," I said honestly. "I've been sitting for hours. I'll stand."

Lester tilted his head back as if he was peevishly offended. I grimaced behind his back.

"All right, now that we're all here…" The lawyer got out his notes to begin reading.

"Yvonne, darling, it's been forever!" loudly interrupted a woman sitting in one of the front chairs. She was thin and bony, her face stretched over her skull as if it had seen too many chemicals and surgeries. Her hair was so bleached and styled that even a strong wind wouldn't have budged it. She beckoned for me to go hug her. Pearls and gold dangled from her wrists.

I waved back awkwardly to Juliet, but stayed where I was. "Yep."

Juliet made a pouty face, and her red lipstick reminded me of a clown. "Ah, come say hello to your favorite aunt."

"Actually, we are here to respect Antigone's last will and testament. Mr. Fairworth?" said my mother. I got the impression that it had been very tense in the room before we arrived.

"Yes, let us begin," said the lawyer, who began reading the legal preamble. I bounced back and forth on my heels and toes, both because it was extremely boring and because I was incredibly tired and overcaffeinated. Out of the corner of my eye, I saw Lester Harrow looking at me.

I looked back at him, and he smiled coyly. I furrowed my eyebrows and gestured What? He turned back around, grinning with self-satisfaction.

Mom was right; the Harrows are weird.

Leandra Meadowlark

Juliet's perfume still smelled cheap, and her short stint in prison had taken away something of the confident air that she was known for. Her husband had died in prison, and I wasn't sorry about it.

Bjorn looked beaten down, as if he'd had to work really hard to get out of bed that morning and his shabby suit had been pulled out of the closet for the first time in years. Lester looked stiff, confident, and aloof, as always, but now he also looked angry. He alone held something of the arrogance I remembered of the Harrows.

It was a relief when Yvonne and Olivia entered the room, because Juliet would not stop staring at me. Now that the lawyer was reading the will, they weren't looking at me anymore.

Juliet made me feel like I needed to take a shower in acid, but I knew it wouldn't help.

The lawyer read off a list of possessions my mother had had. It had taken this long for the will to be read for reasons I never wanted to understand, except that the words "police report," "conflicting interests," "forgery," and "probate" were used a lot. At one point, I had hoped some of Mom's inheritance from her father would come down to me, so I could pay for college and travel a bit. Those hopes were dashed when I learned that Juliet had used up that inheritance long before my mother had died.

The fan on the lawyer's computer was humming loudly, and I found a deep bass line in it. I tapped my fingers against my pocket, keeping rhythm with the tune in my head.

I had some possessions of Mom's stashed away in Beatrice's closet, things that she had left with Dad before she left him and took me to Winter Hill, some old toys and clothes I didn't much care for. I hadn't looked in the box in years.

I remembered the little white room full of books Mom and I had shared with Tori. The thought of the books had grown with me over the years, the hundreds of books we had stacked in that little room. I didn't know if they even existed anymore. I had found some of the titles and stored them on my e-reader.

I was curious about the fate of the books, but I didn't want the Harrows thinking I wanted them. If they knew that, they would do everything they could to destroy them.

The list of my mother's possessions was short: a box of clothes, some trinkets that had been in her room at Winter Hill, and a small sum of money in a savings account that was all that was left after Juliet's frivolous spending.

"A total of $84.16, to Leandra Meadowlark, to use for school and her future," said the lawyer.

I didn't give Juliet the satisfaction of looking upset when she looked back at me expectantly. I was surprised there was anything left at all, but the final numbers burned a newfound hatred for Juliet into my stomach. Dad stiffened at my side as well.

"And the property of 472 books," the lawyer concluded, "currently in the possession of the state, is to be left to Yvonne Meadowlark, now Yvonne Rainier."

Yvonne Meadowlark Rainier

Everyone turned to look at me, and I felt like putting my hands up and exclaiming "I didn't do it!" Instead, I cleared my throat and said, "Books?"

"Yes," said the lawyer. "Quite a few of them."

"Are you sure they aren't supposed to go to Leandra?" I asked, looking sideways at my cousin.

Her face was expressionless; she was looking, deadpan, at the lawyer.

"No, I'm afraid the will is quite clear on this," said Mr. Fairbanks. "The books, all registered and titled here, go to you."

"And nothing was left for Tori Harrow?" asked Juliet.

The lawyer frowned, "No, ma'am, nothing for anyone named Tori Harrow."

"She could have a different last name now," she prompted. "No one tells me anything about my beloved daughter," she added dramatically.

Leandra snorted. The Harrows glared at her.

"No, I'm afraid nothing was left for a Tori, Harrow or otherwise," said the lawyer.

This visibly distressed Juliet. Mother fidgeted beside me. I looked at her and wondered what she might be thinking.

"Well, ladies and gentlemen." Mr. Fairbanks tapped the papers on the table. "That is it."

Leandra Meadowlark

I ran out into the cold before anyone else, walking quickly back to Dad's Bronco. I knew it was a bad idea to get separated from Dad, but I had to get away from that room and everything in it. The fresh air helped, but only a little.

Marvin was sitting in his truck across the road. I waved to him.

My head pounded with old anger and resentment. Yvonne was left the books? Why? Why did Mom think her cousin deserved all the books instead of me? All the books I had read to Tori? The fact that Mom had left them to someone else...

My eyes caught something grey gliding across the parking lot. I looked up and caught sight of a ghost skating around the side of the building. She stopped suddenly, her long skirt flaring out. She looked at me and smiled. I had never seen a ghost so clearly. She looked like a clip from a black-and-white film superimposed onto reality. She waved for me to come after her and skated across the lawn to the back of the building.

I scanned the parking lot and then followed her.

She was nowhere to be seen behind the building, which was just a grassy lot. A road separated the grass from another building complex.

I searched for the roller-skating ghost for a moment, and I wondered why so many people were slowly walking down the road in the cold. Hundreds of people. Why weren't they all wearing coats?

I stopped and stared. Some of them still had color, so it took me a moment to realize that the hundreds of bodies meandering slowly down the road were ghosts. I had never seen so many ghosts in one place. What were they doing there?

"You can see them," said Bjorn coldly. I jumped. His eyes were the same steely grey as the rest of the Harrows'. "I knew you could," he whispered angrily.

"Hello cousin," said Lester Harrow, walking up behind his brother. "Been a while. Lots to catch up on."

"Yeah, how was prison?" I said, turning slowly. I was out of view of the parking lot, and Lester and Bjorn blocked the easy way back.

"The TV special of Winter Hill is out," said Lester, holding up a DVD, still in the wrapping. The girl on the cover, who played me, was looking up at the sky, bright eyed and vulnerable. Lester looked at the cover and shook his head. "Small, whiny little bitch. She looks just like you."

He threw the movie at my feet. The director had sent me the script. I had read it in under an hour. It was dramatic, tragic, heart wrenching, and nothing like what actually happened. They had changed our names and picked actresses who looked nothing like Tori or me, despite what Lester thought. Beatrice had watched it, then called to tell me it was ridiculous, "but they got the Harrows about right." She had chucked darkly.

"Did you like your part?" I said, unfazed. "I do enjoy getting royalty checks for it."

Lester grimaced. Bjorn looked sideways at his brother. They hadn't watched it, just picked it up from a bargain bin at the drugstore to torment me.

"You think you're a hero?" asked Lester, nodding to the film at my feet. "All those little girls watching. I wonder what they would say if they knew how much you screamed when—"

I took a deep breath and clenched my teeth hard, drowning out what he had to say. I turned away from them to go back to the parking lot, but in such a way that I could keep my eye on them.

They watched me go, and I felt the prickle of fear that I remembered from Winter Hill.

"She knows," said Bjorn. "She knows you can see the ghosts."

"I don't care what that woman thinks," I growled.

"You could have saved her!" Bjorn shouted, walking up behind me. I turned abruptly and held my ground. He looked exactly like I remembered him, just a bit older, like I was...but I was also taller than I used to be.

Bjorn was seething, and I remembered the viciousness of the Harrows; I remembered the sporadic, vicious way they fought. I called it the red haze, because all you see is red until you snap out of it with a shaking body, wondering what just happened.

Bjorn fumed, with a hint of desperation, "Tell me right now if you can really see ghosts." I could see the scar on his nose from when his dad had pushed him down the stairs.

"I have nothing to say to you," I said darkly.

Bjorn shook his head. "Tell me right now, because if you can, then my sister is dead because of you."

My face became blank, and I hardly remember uttering the words, "Tori's not dead," before I began to see red. My whole body clenched up, and I was lost to a rage I shared with my cousins because we were, in fact, related.

Yvonne Meadowlark Rainier

"Silis!" I shouted after my dog, who was so upset that he had scratched up the door panel. When I got the door open, he bolted around the side of the building like a greyhound. I rounded the corner after him just in time to see Bjorn and Leandra brawling viciously.

Lester stepped in, pulled on the back of Leandra's coat with two hands, and threw her to the ground hard. Silis leapt over Leandra and sank his sharp Doberman teeth into Bjorn's arm.

"Silis, down!" I shouted and pulled him away. He let go reluctantly, but snarled and pulled against me. I looked back at Leandra, who got up stiffly and watched the two boys warily. She was breathing hard and shaking. She had a bruise appearing on her jaw.

"What the hell is this?" I said angrily. "Did you attack her?!"

Bjorn held his wrist. His suit sleeve was completely in tatters. "None of your fucking business!"

"Excuse me?" I said incredulously, but before I could go over and help Silis finish the job, I heard a car door shut. It was a grey Porsche parked on the street nearby.

Juliet strutted over. "Such vulgarity! You ladies should watch your manners."

"This is assault!" I shouted. "These little shits are going to jail."

"Yes?" said Juliet, clapping her hands together nonchalantly. "I'm sure the police would love to hear about your dog attacking my sons. I'm certain the penalty for any canine attacking a person is execution."

My stomach dropped ten stories.

"Silence, Juliet," said my mother sternly, marching up regally behind us. A man was running close behind her. "Your drivel is as banal as it is ludicrous."

"I'm fine, Marvin," said Leandra darkly as the man inspected her.

Before Marvin could round on the boys, Mom confronted Bjorn. Before he could protest, she grabbed his wrist and pulled up the tattered sleeve of his suit jacket. He winced at the movement, but it was clear that his arm was unscathed. Silis had only bitten his jacket.

"Hum," tutted Mom, and she went over to Silis and patted him on the head affectionately. "Good dog."

"Well," said Juliet breathily, "I'm sure you all have had a fine laugh at my son for defending himself against this girl, but we will have no choice but to have your dog reported, impounded—"

"I watched Bjorn and Lester attack Leandra," I said sternly. "I'm calling the police and having them both arrested, and you arrested for covering it up!"

"Would that be before or after they take your dog for attacking a human?" asked Juliet impishly. "Because I assure you, dear child, that would occur long before any such far-fetched accusations were pressed against my boys. Can you for certain dictate that it was not Leandra who attacked first?"

Before I could reply, Leandra laughed dryly, sounding very calm for a girl who was bleeding profusely from her nose and lips. I hadn't noticed Mom walk over to check on her. Marvin stared daggers at the boys.

"That's a great idea, Juliet; tell all your friends at the police station that your son got his ass kicked by me," said Leandra.

Leandra Meadowlark

I wiped the blood off my face and sniffed, regretting it almost instantly. Bloody noses sting, and I hate the way they taste. Olivia and Marvin kept coming near me to look at my face, and I kept stepping away.

"Silis nipped him, maybe!" said Yvonne.

"That's a lot of blood for just a nip," scoffed Juliet.

"That's from his face," I said coolly, remembering the solid hit I'd landed on his jaw with my elbow. I hoped his teeth ripped apart his mouth, and that it took forever to heal, like he used to do to me. "You're getting senile in your old age, auntie."

Olivia laughed heartily.

Bjorn pulled out his phone and started recording us, so I pulled out mine and did the same.

"Look at Bjorn, everyone," I said loudly. "Nice split lip. Would you like to tell everyone how you got it?"

"You'll pay for everything, Leandra," snarled Bjorn.

"Not before I royally fuck up the remainder of your life," I said coldly. I'd studied law in college and knew police protocol and forensics. I wasn't the same scared little girl I used to be. "Want me to bring new evidence in the Justinia Ingrid case?"

"You have nothing to threaten us with there, my dear girl," said Juliet patronizingly.

I turned my phone to her. "I haven't been rotting in prison like some of you, Juliet. I'm ready for another round of media bouts if you are."

"Poor little Leandra," sighed Juliet. "Did that sailor's wife teach you to be so foul mouthed? I had hoped the state would find someone better for you."

"Hey!" shouted Yvonne. Silis growled. "That's enough!"

"Darling." Juliet held up her hand to silence her.

"Don't you 'darling' me!" Yvonne stormed, marching right up into Juliet's face, Silis pulling on his collar and growling deeply. Juliet looked profoundly taken aback. "I have a lawyer, and I have connections, and I will get shit raining down on you so hard—"

"Social media time, I think," I said, still recording, "Hashtag Winter Hill, hashtag ambulance, hashtag retrial."

"Time to leave, Juliet," said Olivia sternly.

Juliet scoffed, but Silis's growl was becoming impressively formidable. His ears were back and his hackles were raised.

Juliet walked back to the car, somehow making it look as if it was her idea.

Bjorn and Lester followed; Lester looked back and waved at my video. "Cute, Leandra."

"Don't talk to Leandra!" snapped Yvonne. "You cantankerous little—!"

"Such strong words from women who failed to keep their husbands alive," said Juliet before closing the door of her car.

Yvonne bristled visibly. I looked back on instinct and saw Dad rounding the front of the building with Mr. Fairbanks. He took one look at me and sprinted over.

I turned to Bjorn and Lester. "You better run," I said, wiping blood off my face. "He looks pissed."

Stitched

Yvonne Meadowlark Rainier

"I can't BELIEVE this!" I blustered, walking Silis with Mom outside the hospital. "They aren't going to charge them with anything?"

"No, Gerald isn't going to press any charges," said Mom calmly.

"Why?" I almost hit my head on a low hanging branch. "They assaulted Leandra!" It was still cold outside, but I was so angry, it actually felt good.

"They did," said Mom, "and the authorities have been notified, and action will be taken, but you have to understand how Juliet and the Harrows work." Mom sat on one of the nice benches and began scrolling through her tablet. "Juliet is an extremely manipulative woman. It would not be her who was charged, it would be her sons."

"Yeah! Isn't that the point?"

"For her, yes," said Mom, "and by no means am I defending them or their actions, Yvonne, but to put it bluntly, Juliet wanted this to happen." Mom put on her reading glasses and began sifting through her contact list. "Which means we will not go along with it."

"Legit," I conceded, remembering some distasteful stories of others Juliet had manipulated in the cult. "But..."

"She was counting on Gerald to defend Leandra. She wanted him to fight the boys."

"Just— Why?" I asked, scratching Silis's head. "I don't get why they would do anything like this."

"We've all been wondering the same thing for years, Baby Daisy." Mom tapped keys on her tablet in quick succession. "And I know it's difficult, because you are a wonderfully fiery and protective spirit, but think also for the well-being of those boys."

"Why?" I said incredulously. "You saw what they did!"

"I also saw what Leandra did to Bjorn," said Mom, who cocked her head in approval. "Girl knows how to take care of herself. I'm so glad Beatrice was there for her."

"Who was Beatrice again?" I asked, rubbing my fingers together inside my jacket. "Was she the nice gal who watched Leandra? The navy SEAL?"

"Mmmhmm," said Mom.

"Oh, I liked her." I remembered meeting her briefly many years ago. "She had the best attitude."

"Yes, she did. She passed away last night, I'm afraid," Mom said regretfully.

"Really? Is that why Leandra was here?"

"Yes, she Chimed for her this morning."

"Oh, wow." I scratched my neck. "Poor girl. And I was complaining about driving."

"She's had a hard life, and a harder day," said Mom, "though Gerald says she is taking it well, considering."

"It's so cool that she picked up the Chime. I remember when Gerald came to Chime for Richard when he was stuck in the Fleetwood. He played all of Richard's favorite songs. Richard really liked it." It was getting easier to talk about Richard. After his ghost crossed over, things had gotten better. It still sucked, but it was better. "What does she use? Gerald used a harmonica."

"She does too," said Mom. "The same one Granddad gave him."

"Aw, that's cool." There weren't very many Chimes left that people knew of. "What does Gerald do for a living?"

"Besides being a Chime?" said Olivia. "Construction, here and there. House painting, freelance work. The Chime is not known to be a lucrative occupation."

"Then why did Juliet want him at Winter Hill?" I said.

Mom gave me a look, as if I was asking questions I shouldn't, but answered, "I suspect it was more to keep Antigone near her than anything. He was not there long."

"But if you think about it, their cult had some weird thing to do with keeping ghosts around, and Chimers make them go away. It doesn't make sense."

"Do you want to understand those people?" Mom asked.

"Not really," I said. "What are you doing?" I looked at the brightly colored picture on her tablet.

"I'm ordering flowers for Beatrice's memorial." She showed me a few arrangements.

"Aw, that's nice," I said, pointing to the one that looked most like Grandma Lilly's garden. I looked up at the windows of the hospital. "I hope Leandra's OK."

"That's a very fine thing for you to hope, my dear," said Mom. "And I'm sure she appreciated you standing up for her."

I looked skeptical. "I don't think that's what she felt, Mom."

Mom chuckled. "Well, you can be a little bossy."

"Darn tootin'," I said as Silis rolled in the cold November grass, very pleased with himself.

Leandra Meadowlark

I shouldn't have snapped at Yvonne, but I knew I wasn't that bad. I pulled on my coat gingerly. There was still blood on it. I'd have to wash it out later. They took an X-ray of my side to make sure no fluid was building up in my chest cavity, but didn't find anything serious, as I knew they wouldn't.

I'd suffered worse.

"He slammed you to the ground. You could have a concussion!" Yvonne had said with concern. "There's an urgent care just around—"

"I don't need your help!" I had shouted before storming back to the Bronco. Dad didn't say anything when he got in. He was so furious, I'm not sure he could speak. I waved for him to go, and he set out for the hospital with as much gusto as the old Ford Bronco could muster.

I really didn't want to go to the ER. I wanted to run away and curl up in a hole somewhere. I wanted to go back to school and sink into the books of the library, or find a drum set and rip it to shreds, but I knew what that would do to Dad, so I tolerated nurses and doctors and people in the waiting rooms staring at us. They tried to get me to sit in a wheelchair, but I walked defiantly. I don't like wheelchairs.

The first thing I did was throw up in the trash can in the admitting room, because Yvonne was right; I had a concussion. I felt much better after throwing up and knew that the worst of the concussion was over. The nausea was nothing a Benadryl couldn't take away.

They had put two butterfly bandages on my scalp and taken the X-rays of my ribs. I waited for the results to come back as an annoying nurse tried to get me to talk about what had happened, while Dad was getting his wrist looked at. The other doctors and nurses hadn't bothered me, but this nurse was a young woman who continued to ask me vague questions in an increasingly soft voice, expressing that there were many resources available for women in difficult situations.

Today already sucked. I wanted to get out of Rockhouse and go back to school. I wanted to go back to my projects and books. Most of all, I wanted to get away from this nurse's pity. I hate pity.

Dad walked into my pastel-colored room with a fresh bandage around his wrist. He had tried to open the car doors as Juliet, Bjorn, and Lester were speeding off, but had fallen onto the pavement. Lester drove away in a panic. Olivia convinced Dad on the way to the Bronco not to follow them because I needed to be taken to the hospital immediately. The truth was we both needed the hospital, and neither one of us would benefit from following the Harrows.

"How are you?" he asked.

"Fine," I said. "You?"

"Fine," he said, waving his wrist.

The nurse gave him a suspicious look, and I lost it.

"You should probably go," Dad said to the nurse as I stormed at her. She left quickly with a shocked look on her face.

Dad sighed and I mumbled as I sorted through the sack of items they were sending home with me.

I looked down at Dad's wrist. "You get stitched?

"Just some butterfly bandages and a round of antibiotics," he said, grinning. That was his defense, his boyish grin. I sat up straighter to look tough. He didn't need to see me like this today.

"I'm kind of relieved," I said, trying to change the conversation. "I knew something was going to happen today; now it's happened. It's over." I grinned back at him.

"Yeah." Dad looked down and scratched his wrist absently.

"Is everything done with the will?" I said, trying to distract him. "Is all of it done now?"

"Yep," said Dad, and he pulled out an envelope from his jacket and handed it to me. "Your check."

I opened the envelope and looked at the tiny sum printed neatly on the page. Mom and Juliet had inherited a more than comfortable amount of money from their parents. When Mom went back to the cult, Juliet took over her account.

"They spent everything," I said sadly.

"I'm sorry," Dad said quietly. I looked up, and my dad's boyish face was breaking down. This was a hard day we both had been waiting for and dreading. There we were, in a hospital room, and it felt like the right place to be.

"It's OK," I said, pocketing the check and grinning at him again. "I don't need it. They're just assholes, not worth my time."

We both smiled reassuringly at each other, but our hearts ached. There was nothing I could say to relieve his guilt, and nothing he could do to end mine.

"Your doctor said you have to breathe into a device?" he said.

"Yeah, this thing." I held up what the respiratory therapist had called an "incentive spirometer." It was a strange plastic contraption I had to blow into every hour for the next six to eight weeks. "Keeps the fluid from building up in my lungs."

"Looks like a ph tester for a hot tub," he said.

"Yeah." I laughed, but stopped immediately because it hurt.

Dad pulled out his phone. "Olivia and Yvonne are waiting outside. They want to know if we want any food."

"What?" I said, though I didn't need him to repeat it. "Why do they want to get us food?"

Dad shrugged. "To catch up. They said they'd understand if you don't feel up to it."

"Do you want to?" I asked.

"It's up to you," he said.

I hated it when he answered like that. What it really meant was that he wanted to, but didn't want to push it on me.

"Yeah, sure." I said. "Whatever."

Dad started texting. I gathered my bag of medical swag.

Yvonne Meadowlark Rainier

"What do you feel like eating?" Mom asked, looking up from her phone.

"Chinese," I said with gusto. "But you know, whatever."

Olivia raised an eyebrow but responded dutifully.

Leandra Meadowlark

"How about Chinese?" asked Dad, texting as we waited for the slow glass doors to open. He had already checked us out.

"Sure. I want pot stickers," I said, relieved because I wanted to eat a lot of food and because the Harrows abhorred Asian food.

Dad grinned in amusement as he texted Olivia back.

"What?" I asked, squinting into the sunlight outside.

"Nothing," he said.

MYTHS

Leandra Meadowlark

The small room I shared with Tori and Mom at Winter Hill was full of books and not much else. There were so many books, we could make forts with them. I read them all, and when things got really bad, I locked the door, shoved a blanket under it, and read Tori stories out loud. I never let her be the closest one to the door, in case they came in to take one of us away.

I don't remember them ever saying they would do that, but I always had the feeling it would happen if I looked away. So I made sure I was always between Tori and the door.

"How are you so stable? How are you so collected?" one psychologist had asked me. He had flown down to do a study on me for his research on cult logic not long after the media storm about Winter Hill.

"Because I knew they were wrong," I told him, tapping my toes in my shoes. I had a great tune thought up in my head and I really wanted to go write it down. I could hear the bass in the buzz of the neon lights and trilling piccolo in the hum of the air conditioning.

Buzzut tut tut, buzzut tut tut.

That didn't seem to satisfy him. "But how did you know?" he asked in a quieter tone, as if asking the question more softly would make it less repetitive. "Did you have a role model? Did you, perhaps, find solace in the concept of a higher power?"

"Like what?" I asked quickly, trying to keep the rhythm of the tune; I really wished I could go home and record it on the old tape recorder Beatrice had given me.

Buzzut ta-da tut tut, buzzut ta-da tut tut.

"Like God, Jesus, Buddha?"

The silence carried on for a while as I thought of a particularly intricate drumbeat. The psychologist must have taken it for contemplation, because he sounded strangely quiet when he said, "Maybe even the deity your aunt worshiped?"

I stopped tapping my toes, and I lost the sound of the music. It fell away like a rock falling from a cliff, and suddenly I was sitting in a room with an annoying buzzing neon light and an old broken air conditioner. Did he even understand what he was asking me? "I came out so rational because I'm not stupid enough to believe in someone else's notion of a god," I said flatly.

"So, you don't believe in God?" he asked inquisitively. "You don't think your mother went to heaven?"

"That's none of your business," said my dad threateningly. I'd forgotten he was in the room, standing back in the shadows. He was good at being invisible. The psychologist seemed to have forgotten about his presence as well, because he fidgeted nervously and changed his demeanor entirely when my dad asked him, "Are you done?"

"One last thing," he said, leaning forward and looking at me in earnest. "I lost my mother when I was very young too. How are you doing with it?"

I gave him the expressionless stare I had used for years on my aunt and the others at Winter Hill. My mother had died in the same bed I shared with her and Tori. I had called for help and no one had come. They said I was just emotional, that I just wanted attention. The ones who could have helped didn't want to hear me scream that something was very wrong with my mother.

Why were they only taking an interest now?

The first week away from Winter Hill, I bought a cheap bottle of hair dye and some scissors at the dollar store. Two weeks later, I had a ring in my nose and one in my eyebrow. I outlined my eyes in black to make them stand out. I wanted all the social workers and teachers to look me in the eye when they told me I was brave, or sick, or emotional, or whatever else they had to say. It all meant the same thing to me, and I wanted them to see that I didn't care, because they had done absolutely nothing to help my mother, Tori, or me when it really mattered.

I had saved myself, and I had suffered for it. All these people pretending to help me after the fact just wanted to make themselves feel better.

I knew I didn't have to answer the psychologist sitting in front of me, and I certainly didn't have to listen to him. I had only agreed to meet him because he said something in his letter about the research helping other people. I felt like an idiot for believing him, but mostly I was pissed off because his stupid question made me lose my drumbeat. Music could actually help people, and because of him, I had lost it.

I had saved myself. With the Chime, I could help others. To me, that's all that mattered.

"I'm fine with it," I said darkly. "Are you?"

Yvonne Meadowlark Rainier

Mom and I got everyone Chinese food because that seemed like the right thing to do on a shitty day like this.

We met Leandra and Martin at their house with several bags of delicious-smelling takeout. Mom drove so I could fend off the drooling Doberman.

We pulled up next to Martin's old Chevy truck in the driveway. Gerald had parked his Bronco on the street for us. Martin met us and helped carry in the food, and I made sure Silis was leashed before I let him rampage around.

Gerald held open the screen door for us. The house was vaguely familiar.

"The last time you were here was the family reunion, wasn't it?" asked Gerald as Mom pulled Styrofoam containers from the plastic bags and Martin retrieved a pile of plates.

"Yeah! Been a while," I said, finding a suitable place in the living room for Silis to lie down and behave himself.

Leandra was sitting at the round kitchen table with notebooks, her tablet with a keyboard, and pencils and highlighters. She hardly looked up from her studies.

"How you doin'?" I inquired somewhat hesitantly. I half expected her to start shouting at me again. Instead, she closed down her tablet and stacked it neatly on her notebooks.

"I'm hungry," she said decisively.

Martin, Mom, and Gerald sat on the sofas in the living room and talked about all sorts of things I had no connection to whatsoever. I sat on the other side of the table to keep an eye on Silis, who liked to sniff around people's plates. I didn't mind being left out of the conversation; I was too busy stuffing my face with sesame beef, pot stickers, and heaps of fried rice. All I'd had to eat that day was crappy food filled with sugar and caffeine. Real food tasted delicious.

Leandra's attitude was about the same, and though she had piled her plate twice as high as I had, she was already almost done.

My phone beeped, and I checked my text messages. Mom's rang at the same time. Janis had sent us a picture of a goofily grinning baby Timmy with a bow on his head.

"Daw, goob," I said as Mom showed her grandson off to Gerald and Martin. I showed the picture to Leandra. "That's Timmy, my new nephew."

Leandra grinned a bit. "Tim the Enchanter."

"Oh yes, he's very enchanting," said Mom.

Leandra and I looked at each other. Fortunately, I understood the Monty Python reference my mother did not. I put two fingers in front of my face and said "Nasty, big, pointy teeth!"

Leandra snorted and went back to reading her tablet. I wanted to know what she was doing, but didn't want to start asking her a bunch of awkward questions.

That didn't last.

"Who are you talking to?" I asked finally.

She looked up, as if surprised I was talking to her. "No one," she said.

"Playing games?" I said. "I love phone games."

"No, I'm reading."

"What are you reading?" I asked curiously. She had been typing a lot to be reading.

She hesitated before responding. "Articles. Websites. First it was a quote from Aristotle that led to an article about an artist that was inspired by Dumas, and then it went to a mathematical question that some believe to be the formula for the best Latin drum rhythm, and now I'm reading bits of The Count of Monte Cristo."

"Oh," I said, looking down at Silis. "That's cool."

Leandra ate a few more bites of Mother's Chicken.

"I can't remember if I've read The Count of Monte Cristo," I said.

"You'd remember," said Leandra. "It's about 1,400 pages."

"Um, wow," I said, "That's bigger than Harry Potter, huh?"

Leandra nodded. "Yeah, it is."

"I love Harry Potter," I said, trying to find some sort of common ground for conversation. "Gryffindor!"

Leandra looked sideways at me.

"What?" I said.

"I never read those."

I was floored. "You've never read Harry Potter?"

"No," she said flatly.

"Why?" I demanded. I had woken up at four in the morning to wait in line at the bookstore to get the last three books. The fact that I was an adult and it was a kid's book series was hugely irrelevant. It was Harry Potter. "You'll read The Count of Monte Cristo, but not Harry Potter?"

Leandra shrugged and went back to reading. I sat back and slurped the last of my soda loudly.

"What?" said Leandra irritably.

"Nothing," I said, squinting one eye for effect. "I'm just silently judging your choice of literature."

Leandra looked like she couldn't decide whether to be angry or laugh.

"Don't laugh," I said, "it'll make your ribs hurt."

"Nah," said Leandra. "Sneezing is what gets you."

"Oh, I bet." I leaned down and scratched Silis's head. "Watch out for the killer sneezles!"

Silis sneezed, and I tried not to laugh so Leandra wouldn't laugh. Us both trying not to laugh was much more difficult than I thought, so I cleared my throat and picked up some coins off the table.

"These are neat," I said, spinning the gold dollars across the tabletop. One tinged loudly against a water glass, and I grimaced. "It's not broken, I swear."

Leandra smirked and took two gold dollars from a small pile on the table. "These are the best ones."

"For what?" I said.

Leandra raised an eyebrow and cleared space on the table. She took a coin in each hand and placed them on top of each other. She stood still for a moment, and I noticed Gerald and Martin had stopped talking. Leandra closed her eyes and nodded four times, then began to tap the coins together in a fast but steady rhythm. The tapping continued until suddenly her fingers were a blur of beats and rhythms. It sounded like a full-blown drum set.

"Wow!" I said when she finished.

"You're getting pretty good," said Martin.

Leandra grinned and slid the coins across the table to me. "Music major."

"Hm," I said, tapping the coins togcthcr, "cool."

"Have you seen this?" Leandra pulled a notebook from under her stack of papers. It was bound with one of those plastic spiral things I remember making books with in grade school. The cover was a photocopy of a very old book that I had to squint to make out, but I recognized one familiar part of it almost immediately.

"The Meadowlark Book of Myths?" I said.

Mom stopped talking and looked over at us. I thumbed through the first few pages. Each page had a photocopy of an old diary, and adjacent to it were handwritten translations and notes.

"What is this?" I said, spotting several references to the Chime, though I couldn't really tell what they were for.

"You haven't seen this?" Leandra sounded surprised, and she turned the pages to one with a blue sticky note on it. That page had a drawing of a raft floating down a wide river.

"It's the diary of Jenkins Meadowlark, and some accounts from his two brothers. It's about the three Meadowlark brothers who studied the Chime."

"Not brothers," said Mom, a touch too tartly. "They were three orphaned children, set adrift on a raft in the Meadowlark River. The town took them in and named them Meadowlark. It's unclear if they were related."

"Yes, but they called themselves brothers," Leandra said as if that settled the matter. I turned to the next page, where there was a crude sketch of a face with two coins over the person's eyes.

Leandra pointed to the sketch. "Know the story of the ferryman on the River Styx?"

"Coins on the eyes as a toll for the ferryman?" I said, looking at a few scribbles Leandra had written in what looked like a strange Morse code.

Leandra nodded, flipping the coins between her fingers.

"Is this real?" I asked, flipping through the rest of the pages.

"Yeah," said Leandra, as if it was a strange question.

I caught the tense look Mom gave Gerald.

"Have you read this, Mom?" I held up the photocopy. "Where's the original?"

"Grandma Lilly has it," said Mom. "It's illuminating, but very...grim. She did not let me read it until I was your age, Yvonne. How did Leandra get a copy?" Mom asked Gerald.

"I asked for it," said Leandra. "You should read it." She nodded to me. "It's part of your history. Your grandma would make you a copy too," she said, as if she were talking about a health book.

"My mother made you a copy?" said Mom thoughtfully, then she nodded in approval and took a sip of tea.

"Is there stuff in there on ghosts?" I asked.

"Ghosts?" said Leandra.

My phone beeped loudly, and so did Mom's. It was another cute picture of Timmy, playing drums with the kitchen pans. Mom shared it with Gerald and Martin enthusiastically, and Leandra went quietly back to her studies, tapping the coins in offhand beats on the table.

After we had all gone back for seconds and thirds, Gerald, Leandra, and Martin saw us off at the Trooper. "Well, we will be staying the night at The Pavilion and leaving again tomorrow," said Mom, giving Gerald a big hug.

"Did you want any of the books, Leandra?" I asked, but was interrupted by a ghost zipping past me. It was the forties girl on roller skates again. She was skating very quickly up the road. She looked back at me briefly, her face full of alarm. She pointed up the hill, then skated off as fast as she could.

"Um, sorry," I said, turning back to Leandra, because I'm sure I must have looked startled. But Leandra was looking over at the roller-skater ghost with the same bewilderment as I was.

"Can you see—" I began.

"We should be off, I think," Mom interrupted, giving me a meaningful look. She reached out for Leandra and said kindly, "I hope we get to see you again before we leave tomorrow, my darling."

Leandra hugged her as if she was out of practice. I wanted to ask her if she could see ghosts, but Mom gave me another "I know something you don't" look, and I let it be.

I smiled and pulled out my phone. "We're picking up the books tomorrow. I'll give you my cell number; text me if there's any books you want, and I'll send them to you. You're welcome to come look through them too, if you want."

"Hm, thanks," said Leandra, and recorded my number in her phone.

"Let's go, my dear," said Mom, pulling on my sleeve.

"What?" I said irritably.

"We need to check in before the hotel salon gets swamped," said Mom dramatically, "It's very important."

I took the hint and said bye to Gerald, Martin, and Leandra.

Leandra was looking back up the hill where the roller-skating ghost had gone. Ghosts usually did strange things, but this felt…urgent.

Leandra's yellow eyes met mine briefly before I set off down the road in the Trooper. I didn't see the roller-skating ghost on our drive to the hotel, but I couldn't shake the feeling that something was very wrong.

Leandra Meadowlark

"Bjorn was upset because Juliet told him some bull about Tori being dead," I said, breathing into the spirometer, holding the little float up for several seconds, then letting it go. "Bjorn blamed me."

"Did he start the fight?" asked Dad, rolling his empty soda can between his palms.

"I don't remember." I fiddled with the spirometer. "Went red."

"Hm," said Dad.

"Where is Tori?" Martin inquired politely.

Dad shrugged. "We don't know."

Martin nodded solemnly.

"She's fine," I said. "Juliet was just stirring up dirt."

Dad looked sideways at me. "Do you know where she is?"

"I know she's fine; that's all I care about."

"You're not going to tell us how you know, either," said Martin.

"Nope." I put down the spirometer and went to the kitchen cupboard to pour myself a bowl of cereal. I was still hungry.

"Crafty Leandra." Gerald put the can down, and a small smile of relief appeared on his face.

"So, Leandra," said Martin carefully, "Beatrice left me in charge of all her things."

I looked up, chewing a big glob of raisins.

"She left you all the things in her room. If you want to go look through them and pick out the things you want, I'll get them set up in a storage unit for you."

I continued to chew a bit and swallowed, feeling a lump in my throat. "You're selling the house?"

Martin nodded.

"Take your time," said Dad, lying across the sofa. "I'm gonna nap."

I nodded and wiped my mouth. "I'll go now."

I ran up the stairs before they could say anything more about it.

I slammed the door.

I stood, breathing hard, in Beatrice's room. I'd never spent much time in there, though there were several instances in which I wanted to. Sometime during the first week, she asked me not to go in her room, so I didn't. She never went in mine either. I had dreamed of looking through her cabinets and drawers at all her memorabilia from around the world.

That excitement was gone.

I was in a room that smelled like her, and the window was open. Probably Martin's doing. There were flags hanging from the walls, all the places she'd visited.

I had prepared for the heartache of hearing Mom's will for years. I had envisioned every possible outcome, some better and some worse than what had happened.

I had not prepared for this. I even knew it was coming, but I didn't want it to.

I sat down on the bed, felt the indent Beatrice had made in her mattress, and looked at the side table. There were a few pictures there; her navy portrait, a long-ago boyfriend she lost overseas, Martin, her parents.

And then there was the picture of me and her sitting on the back porch. It was taken maybe two years after Winter Hill. She was looking smug, and I was sitting with an attitude, but reluctantly smiling. Martin was standing at the sliding-glass door, drinking an iced tea. Dad had taken the picture. We had all gone bowling for my birthday. Beatrice had won.

You gonna to let them see you cry?

I would keep my word; the Harrows wouldn't see me cry. But alone in Beatrice's room, I started sobbing uncontrollably. It hurt my bruised ribs, but it didn't hurt as much as the emptiness threatening to make me disappear.

STAR TRAILS

Yvonne Meadowlark Rainier

Mom was downstairs in the spa; she had ten different appointments scheduled before we even made it to the hotel room. I wasn't in the mood for spa stuff after all the things that had happened that morning and resolved to sit in the hotel room and catch up on bad TV.

I slept for a few hours, thank glob, but Silis woke me up to go outside, and then I was awake. Mom was probably in the middle of her facial, but I was both restless and bored. Even the enticing idea of spending the rest of the evening in my new pajamas couldn't erase the nagging feeling in my gut.

I wrote a note letting Mom know I was going to drive to the park with Silis. I had let him sleep on the foot of my bed, and he was just as anxious to get out of the hotel room as I was.

"You're lucky we found a hotel with a spa that allows doggies, good buddy," I told Silis as we walked down the fancy hallway to the parking lot.

I pulled out my keys to unlock the car, and a grey blur startled me enough to drop them. It was the skating lady from the lawyer's office. She skated through a Subaru, then jumped up onto the grass and continued skating as if it was smooth pavement. She did an impressive swivel around and looked at me. I was about to go talk to her until I saw what it was she had obviously wanted me to see.

I stared at the back road behind the hotel for a long moment, and at the crowds of grey ghosts that were walking steadily into the scenic forest-covered hills behind the hotel.

Someone walking by asked if I was alright. After reassuring the older Japanese couple that I was fine and not having a seizure, and when Silis was done saying hello, I retrieved my keys and we both got into the car. Our destination was no longer the park.

It wasn't a long drive to find the end of the ghosts' trail. It had been getting dark outside when I'd left the hotel, and now the twilight was making the whimsical droves of ghosts look extremely creepy.

I got out of the car with Silis and sidestepped a few ghosts who whooshed by softly. Ghosts were walking everywhere. They didn't seem to notice me; they just walked by if they had somewhere they needed to go.

I followed them off a small path where a Forest Service sign said there was a small waterfall three miles away. I hoped I wouldn't have to walk that far. There was no one else around besides the hundreds of ghosts. I walked up the old rock path slowly with Silis, turning around every few seconds to make sure the eerie figures I saw were all ghosts, with no humans among them. I tried to speak to some of them, but they had no notion that I was there.

Silis barked at a figure approaching from the trees that was definitely not a ghost. I started and shined my flashlight at it. "You scared me!" I said, feeling my heart race like a rabbit's.

"You're the one walking around in the dark," said Leandra, and turned back to the path. "Come over here. Don't worry, there's no one else here." She walked down the path, hands in her jacket pockets. I looked down hesitantly at Silis, then turned my flashlight off and followed her.

There was still enough light for me to see the ghosts slowing and gathering around a pocket of soft earth a bit off the beaten path. Leandra was looking down into a small crater. The ghosts stared into the crater expectantly, but nothing happened.

"It's a meteorite," said Leandra, standing with the ghosts as if they were ordinary people.

"Can you," I asked tentatively, "see them?"

"Not really; they mostly disintegrate when they enter the atmosphere. There's not much of this one left. Probably just little chunks, I expect. Do you have a metal detector?"

"Oh, a metal detector?" I said. "No."

"Shame." Leandra kicked the dirt. "Meteors are worth a lot, especially this one, I think."

She went back down the hill, leaving a dirt trail behind her. I was pretty sure that if I tried to do that, even in daytime, I would have tripped and injured myself. She did it as if it was a stroll down the lane. Then it occurred to me.

"Hey, I'm the only car over there. How did you get here?"

Leandra pointed to her longboard, leaning against a rock.

"You skateboarded up a hill?" I said incredulously.

"No, I walked up the hill," said Leandra.

"That's a lot of walking."

"Yeah." Leandra shrugged. "I'm good at it."

"Mmm-kay, so, why are you here?"

"Probably the same reason as you," said Leandra, tossing me something. I dropped it, because I already had Silis's leash in one hand and my flashlight in the other. "Sorry," she said.

"What is this?" I asked.

"A piece of the meteorite."

"I thought you didn't have a metal detector?"

"I don't." She pointed with her hand still in her coat pocket. "This is from another site, not far from here. I followed them there, too."

"Followed...?" I prompted, doing my best not to give away the secret I wasn't sure if she knew.

Leandra leaned forward. "The ghosts."

"Yes," I said. "So, you see them?"

"Yeah, don't you?"

"Well, yeah, but it's not something just everyone can do, you know. It's some cosmic force that brings it out in you or something, with rituals and magic." I waved my fingers for emphasis.

Leandra looked annoyed.

"I'm kidding. It's a joke."

"Do you have a blanket?" Leandra asked.

"What?" I looked back at the Trooper. "Yeah, I guess. I have a dog blanket. Why?"

"You'll probably need it," Leandra said. "It'll take me a bit to get these guys to go home, and I need your help, and it's going to get colder."

"I'm sorry, I'm helping?" I asked.

"Why else would you be here?" said Leandra.

"I'm like, fifteen years older than you, and I send ghosts across the great and mystical divide for a living. I think you should hold your horses before ordering me around."

Leandra rolled her eyes and ran back up to the crater's edge. Then she looked down into the crater and rubbed her hands together. "You got a magnet?"

"Yeah."

"Can I borrow it?"

"For what?" A ghost walked right by me and scared me. "Why are they even here?"

"It's the meteorite," said Leandra "I think they thought it was a star."

"A star?" I said, and looked up into the indigo sky, littered with stars. "Oh, that actually makes a lot of sense. But why are they following a meteorite instead of a star?"

"Same reason most people do, probably," said Leandra vaguely, climbing back down the hill and walking toward the Trooper, rubbing her hands together. "The magnet's in the car, right?"

"Yeah," I said, and followed her toward the Trooper.

Silis trotted up to Leandra and sniffed her fervently; she put down one of her hands so he could smell it better. "Hey dog," she said. Silis snorted and trotted away.

I pulled out the old bottle opener magnet stuck to the inside of the glove box. It had come with the car when I'd bought it used. Never thought I'd need it for ghost stuff.

"What do you call ghost work?" I said, handing her the magnet.

"What?"

"This work," I waved at the steady stream of wandering ghosts, then waved back at Leandra, "and your Chime thing; what do you call it?"

Leandra fiddled with the magnet and started back toward the crater. "Well, the Chime is just the Chime, and I've never met anyone else who sees ghosts." She laughed darkly and looked down. "At least, not for real."

"Huh," I said, stumped. "Me neither."

"You comin'?" she said.

"What do you need me for, exactly?"

Leandra shrugged and continued up the hill. I realized she didn't have a flashlight. I watched her go up the hill for a minute before rolling my eyes and getting in the car.

"Better help her out, buddy," I told Silis as I turned the car on. Instead of following her with the flashlight, I drove closer to the crater so the headlights would help illuminate the area. It was probably illegal, but we were doing ghost work (until I found a more exciting name, it would just have to sound official enough). Driving through ghosts is weird, by the way, and yes, they do notice.

It didn't take Leandra long to find the meteorite, surprisingly. She got in the passenger's seat and showed me a small bit of rock stuck to the magnet. The ghosts looked around, strangely confused. A few of them spotted the meteorite through the windshield and began to saunter toward it.

"Yeah, we're leaving," I said, backing up to the parking lot.

"Probably smart," said Leandra. "But it's not like they can hurt us."

"No, but it's frickin' creepy," I said, pulling around and circling back to the main road. The ghosts walked slowly after us. I knew they would catch up in time, but I found myself stepping on the gas pedal more heavily than I normally would have. Those ghosts creeped me out.

Sometimes I am asked if it can be dangerous to Chime.

The most memorable case I can present happened at an old battlefield outside Gettysburg. A local claimed the spirit of a young drummer boy walked the road every night, leading the souls of the dead to the dawn one by one.

I traveled there at once and waited patiently for him to appear. I did not have to wait long, for he appeared just as the sun crested the treetops. I asked him why he came, morning after morning, day after day.

He said, "There's a lot of ghosts out here, and I only know one song to play. One more over, day by day."

Why not learn a new song? Why not lead them away with a grand orchestra? The drummer boy was a ghost. He could not learn a new song.

I went back to Chime at noon, playing my banjo. I saw ghosts come to look, but they all retreated to the shadows of the trees.

I was not their drummer boy.

How much of what we do is belief? How much of what we do is for ourselves? The soldiers were not impressed by my attempts, I tell you.

From the trees, their eerie, rotted figures told me to leave and never return.

I heeded them.

– Meadowlark Book of Myths

Ouroboros

Yvonne Meadowlark Rainier

"So, now where to?" I asked, driving back down the road.

"The house," said Leandra. "I've got to show these to Dad." She was already texting him.

"OK, tell me how to get there when we get back to Rockhouse," I said. "Why didn't you do the Chime there for the ghosts?"

"Probably wouldn't have worked," said Leandra, tapping her feet to some tune in her head. "I'll have to figure out a good place and a good tune for that many people."

"Hm," I said, curious about the Chime. Leandra was studiously typing, so I held in my questions.

My phone, sitting in the charger, beeped, and I looked down at it. It was a short message in all caps. A few seconds later it beeped again, and then again.

"Jeez, what's that about?" I said.

Leandra's phone began to beep as well. "Turn right?" she said, reading the message. Her phone beeped again, and so did mine. "Turn right," Leandra said more firmly.

There was one road sign lit up in green by my headlights a half mile down the road. "White Road," it said. "Who are my messages from?" I asked.

Leandra snatched up my phone and read the contact above the repeated messages. "Janis."

I braked hard and turned right. We drove for a few hundred feet before I pulled off and looked through the messages on my phone. Suddenly they stopped coming in as "TURN RIGHT" and became "CALL ME."

I speed-dialed my sister Janis. "Janis! What?"

"Yvonne, you have to keep driving!" said Janis in a panicked voice. "Someone's going to take Timmy!"

The conversation wasn't long, as Janis insisted I keep driving. "You have to keep driving. I'll call Mom and tell her what's going on, but please keep driving!" she said.

"I'm going, but what about Tim?" I asked, getting my car in gear.

"He's fine, he's with me and Mark at Darcy's house. He'll be safe as long as you get there in time."

"Where?" I asked.

"I'm not sure," she said shakily, "but it's down that road. I didn't have time to check where it goes."

"I know where we're going," said Leandra. "Janis, Tim can see ghosts, can't he?" She said it loud enough for Janis to hear.

"What?" said Janis, "I don't—" I heard her inhale sharply; then she said, "Maybe!"

"Keep Tim away from strangers," said Leandra loudly. In a quieter voice, she said to me in earnest, "You better drive faster. It's a ways away."

"Janis, did you call the cops?" I said urgently.

"I don't know enough to tell them anything," said Janis frantically.

"What did you see?" I asked.

"It wasn't clear, but I saw your car in front of a gate near White Road. Then, inside by a fire, a woman was looking at the picture I sent out earlier, and someone said 'Bring him here. He's the one like smoke.'"

"Call my dad first, Janis. Tell him everything you just told us," Leandra said, and read off his phone number.

"How did you know where I was?" I said.

"You left your navigation settings on in your phone. I hacked it. Sorry," said Janis.

"That's...OK," I said, slightly perturbed by my technology. "Call Gerald and Mom, and we'll keep driving, OK? No one's going to hurt Timmy."

"Thanks, Yva. I love you!"

"You too, sis." I got off the phone with Janis and turned to Leandra, who was bringing up a map on her phone. "Where are we going?"

"Forty-one miles northeast. Dirt road can get us there faster. You have gas?"

"Yeah, three-quarters of a tank. Where are we going?"

"Winter Hill," said Leandra.

"What?" I couldn't hear her over Silis whining in my ear.

Leandra spoke louder. "Winter Hill. The woman she saw was Juliet."

"How do you know?" I said.

"She's said that before, to my cousin Tori, before she tried to kill her."

The Chime is an attempt to fill the silence. It's an empty promise.

Sometimes it hurts more, because the echo can reveal how big the hole is, and most don't want to see it. It's a great responsibility to be a Chime, not only for those we serve, but for ourselves. You can't help someone face their shadows unless you have faced your own.

– Meadowlark Book of Myths

BJORN

Winter Hill was built on a private estate in the mountains. The manor house was large and impressive from the outside, with an earthy feel that made the many guests it housed over the years feel welcome. People paid a great deal for miracle healers and those who claimed they could see the ghosts of their loved ones, and their devotion showed. The gates were ornate wrought iron, an expensive addition that the many patrons of Winter Hill were happy to fund along with several other comforting additions, including a brand-new guest wing.

Bjorn sat in it now, though it did not look nearly as impressive as it had intended to be. The addition to the house was going to be a wing for those who wished to stay and live the way of the Winter Hill Society, as the families of its leaders did. The wing was only half finished when the feds arrested Juliet. Some portraits of the family members still loomed in the dark hallways through the main area, though most were sold off to collectors years ago.

Bjorn looked up at the dilapidated two-by-fours and scaffolding that had been left. He had not slept in two days, since he'd come by briefly to visit. He had a job to go back to, a life he had built precariously since he had been put in foster care. Leandra had her dad, at least. His had died in prison years back. Bjorn had only intended to stay a while, but his mother and brother...

They were still his family.

Bjorn sat and thought mostly about his younger sister, Tori.

"I never said she was dead, foolish boy," Juliet had scolded him on their drive back to Winter Hill. He had been lamenting over the torn sleeve of his one nice coat. Juliet did not even ask if he was all right. In the front seat, Lester and Juliet stared ahead of them. Bjorn could not even remember when he had started calling her Juliet instead of Mother. She had scoffed at him as he wiped blood off his forehead with his tattered sleeve. "I said she was as good as dead. We have important things to do now. Do not get blood on my car seats."

Bjorn shook his head and took a shuddering breath of winter air. As good as dead. That was not what he had heard Juliet say, but she had a way of making him question everything. As soon as they returned to Winter Hill, he pulled his one sweatshirt out of his suitcase to replace his tattered and bloody jacket. His knuckles and arms were bruised from the fight. He was glad for the cold; it distracted him from regret. He had not wanted to fight Leandra. A secret part of him had fantasized that they could become friends again, like they were years and years ago, before either of them knew something was very, very wrong.

He had planned to visit for only an hour or so. It had now been days, and he didn't know when he could leave.

He hated them, but he could not get away.

They were like a spider's web, and the more he flailed, the more trapped he became.

"It's cold out here," said Lester, opening the plastic barrier that kept the weather from entering the rest of the house.

Bjorn didn't say anything.

"Mom's ready. We should go up there," said Lester.

"I don't want to do this," said Bjorn. "I don't want this to be like it was last time."

"It's not! That's the beauty of this, brother. I'm going to go in her stead. She does not have to be here for this. We can do it together."

Bjorn looked up at his older brother with a gaunt face filled with fright and uncertainty.

Lester put a hand on his shoulder. Bjorn tried his best not to flinch away from the loveless touch. "This," he waved to the scaffolding, "means nothing. We can do the real task now, tonight."

"This isn't...right," said Bjorn in a strained voice.

"Ah, don't say that. We agreed on this months ago, all three of us! This is what Tori would have wanted. She would have wanted us to go forward with our lives."

"She was too young," said Bjorn, "and you shouldn't have to go through this either."

Lester laughed darkly. On other occasions, Bjorn would have expected Lester to beat him for saying such things, but tonight Lester just clapped him hard on the shoulder and said, "You and your sympathies."

Bjorn reluctantly followed his brother with heavy steps. He had nowhere else to go.

As Bjorn walked, he was vaguely aware of the many scores of ghosts that circled around him, stuck in the hallways of Winter Hill with a perpetual look of agony. The Winter Hill Society, his mother had called it. It was nothing so romantic. The ghosts were used, like all the other things that came near his mother, used for her own disgusting means. Miracle healing, she called it. With the powers passed down from her family, she could heal almost anyone, she said.

His brother believed it, as did many others they persuaded to join their society with promises of a peaceful afterlife and the story that the mere presence of a Harrow could stave off the effects of an incurable illness. It worked enough that those with money came to believe it, and the money began to flow.

Lester and their mother had been cultivating ghosts for months, using some method they would not discuss with Bjorn. He was all the happier for that; he did not want to know.

They were meeting in his brother's bedroom, where many ghosts stood around a small piece of rock placed on a dirty pedestal made of plaster. The only light came from an open fireplace near the bed. Their mother was there, singing some old song in Latin out of a small black book she kept near her at all times. She smiled at her sons. She hugged and kissed Lester before gesturing for him to sit on the bed. She did the same with Bjorn, though he felt no comfort or warmth in the short embrace.

"Are you ready, my sons?" she asked, as Lester lay back on the red coverlet and removed his tie.

"I am," he said.

She smiled at him and placed the piece of meteorite on his chest. She took a small flask from the pedestal and poured most of its contents into a crystal glass. He toasted them and drank it without hesitation. Bjorn watched with the same vacant expression he had donned for the last ten years.

His family was disgusting, plagued, and vile, and so was he.

Lester fidgeted, coughed, and suddenly lay still. He was not dead, but he soon would be.

Juliet turned to Bjorn. "Are you ready, my son?"

Bjorn didn't do anything, just stared at his brother. Juliet filled the silence by pouring another, smaller glass for him. She set it on the pedestal.

Bjorn sat down stiffly in the chair next to his brother, who was now unconscious on the bed. It would take several minutes for the poison to work, and he had to sit and wait. The grey ghosts around him looked down vaguely at the small piece of meteorite. He turned to the dark liquid on the pedestal and swallowed. His mother eyed him expectantly.

Bjorn picked up the glass and drank it quickly.

Juliet put a cold hand on his arm. She lifted the red and gold flask to her painted lips and drank the rest. "I'll be downstairs," she said. Along with the flask, she placed a revolver on the pedestal. "Do what you must." Juliet left the room.

Once Juliet was far down the hall, Bjorn spit out as much of the liquid as he could into the fireplace, almost burning himself in the process. He looked back at the door, fearful that she had heard him. Several moments passed, and he heard her footsteps fade into nothing.

A large tear fell down Bjorn's quivering face as he felt his mouth burning. He looked imploringly at the blurry figures of the ghosts surrounding them, but he knew there was nothing they could do to help him.

Martian Mountains

Yvonne Meadowlark Rainier

"What does she want to do to Timmy?" I said angrily. "She won't, by the way. She ain't goin' near our Tim. But she apparently wants to try."

"Juliet used to use ghosts for her ritual thing," said Leandra, then added thoughtfully, "Bjorn was never very good at it..."

"Tim's three months old," I said. "How would she know if he could see ghosts? How would she know about him at all?"

"Um..." said Leandra, tapping her fingers on her bag at her feet. "It's complicated, but it doesn't sound like she knows yet. If Janis Saw us going there, perhaps we can stop her before she finds out."

"What madness would be going on?" I said. "Seriously, do I need to pull over and carve a spear or something?"

"No," said Leandra, "but if you do stab them, I wouldn't hold it against you."

"'Them'? Who is 'them' going to be?" I asked.

"Probably just Juliet, Bjorn, and Lester," said Leandra seriously. "I don't think she has any new followers."

"How would we know that?"

"I keep tabs on their social media pages," Leandra said, "among other things."

"You keep tabs on their members?" I said. Silis turned around a few times and got comfortable in the back seat.

Leandra nodded. "They don't stay members for long."

"You're one of those crazy hacker people like my sister, aren't you?" I said.

"You don't have to be a hacker to do things on the internet," said Leandra cryptically.

"So, what's the plan then? Should we be calling the cops? What are we going to do when we get there?" I asked.

"I'm guessing we're going to find out when we go inside," said Leandra stiffly.

"Go inside?" I said. "Why would we be going inside?"

"You just wanna knock and say 'Hey, you can't touch my nephew you don't even know about yet?'" Leandra asked dryly.

"Yeah, now that you mention it, because they can't!" The thought of someone harming my nephews and niece made my stomach drop and my blood boil.

"I don't think we'll be in danger," said Leandra, "but I'm not the one who Saw things."

"OK, OK." I took a deep breath. "Sorry, I'm just a little stressed about this is all."

"I understand," said Leandra. Then, after a bit, she said, "You will be fine."

It was a long drive to Winter Hill, and more so because we couldn't drive as fast as I wanted to along the windy roads up the mountain. I was anxious and scared. I had a gun, but it was at home, locked in Richard's gun safe. Would I need a gun? Should we call the police? It hadn't taken us long to get out of cell range. Our phones had stopped worked shortly after I'd gotten off the phone with Janis. I suddenly wished I had forked over the extra money to get a more expensive coverage plan.

Leandra wasn't saying much, just fiddling in her bag and sticking things in her pockets.

"So, what are you thinking about?" I said, wanting desperately to break the silence.

"What?" said Leandra.

"What are you thinking about? I want a distraction."

"Um, OK. Did you know there are over fifty mountains on Mars?"

"Uh...no, I did not."

"And that Olympus Mons is three times taller than Mt. Everest?"

"Hm."

"The only two open volcanoes on Earth are in South Africa and Antarctica, but the National Science Foundation studies the one in Antarctica because it's safer, what with all the wars at the only other open volcano in Africa. We can see an infinite number of stars and planets and places that will take hundreds of years to reach and explore, but we can't study the volcanoes of our world because we get in the way of our own progress."

"Uh huh."

"It's messed up, in my opinion. People get so stuck in the mess of their own heads that they make rules that block them from going forward. There are things in a drop of ocean water we can't explain, and we can see planets billions of light-years away, but we kill ourselves over fantasies of not dying and living forever. It's stupid." Leandra shook her head. "Even stars die."

"I'm not that big a fan of death," I said dryly. "It's not a happy topic."

Leandra laughed and bit her finger, and then she shook her head and looked back out the window. "Yep."

"What?"

"Nothin'." Leandra shrugged.

"What? You think that because you had an early brush with death, you are some big expert on how everyone should feel about it?" I said.

"See? You didn't want to know." Leandra clipped something to her sleeve.

"What?" I said again.

"You asked me what I'm thinking. You don't want to hear it," Leandra remarked irritably.

"That's not what I— Ugh." I took a breath.

"And quit that," said Leandra.

"What?" I said angrily.

"Stopping because you feel bad for me."

"Stopping what?" I was totally confused, scared, and frustrated.

"You were going to argue, but you stopped because you feel bad for me. I'm not stupid," said Leandra.

"Jesus Christ, I didn't say you were stupid." I fiddled with the heater switches and adjusted the seat unnecessarily to keep my hands busy.

"Just stop," said Leandra. "I don't talk, because it ends up making people mad. Simple. Now we can go on with things." She went back to looking at the meteorite.

"No, we're not done talking," I said. "Let me get this straight. You start every conversation with big, esoteric thoughts like that?"

Leandra rolled her eyes, crossed her arms, and stared out the window. "You asked me what I was thinking. That's what I was thinking. Don't get all pissed off when you get things you asked for."

"I'm not pissed that you told me what you were thinking," I said. "I'm not even pissed off, I'm just irritated that you sound like I should have an opinion on something big like that on the spot."

"I don't! I just told you what I was thinking."

"People must hate you, huh?"

"Yeah, they do. Why?"

"You probably make them feel really dumb," I said honestly. "I have no idea what to say to any of that."

"You don't have to say anything to it. You just wanted to know what I was thinking, and so I told you."

"But I was trying to make conversation so I don't have to think about the fact that I'm going to some crazy person's house with no phone and no weapons or anything. The fact that I'm even concerned that we'd need weapons is terrifying. I just want something to talk about that isn't associated with all that."

"Why?" asked Leandra honestly.

"Because that's what you do when you're in a car with a cousin you don't know very well and you're about to raid her crazy aunt's house who ran a cult and may be plotting to harm your very adorable little nephew!"

"She wouldn't kill him intentionally, she just doesn't care if what she does would kill him," Leandra said in such a matter-of-fact way that I had to turn and look at her.

Leandra seemed to realize that her words sounded callous and cleared her throat. "Look, we'll solve this right now." She grabbed my phone and got past my passcode screen in a few seconds.

"How do you know my passcode?" I said.

"I saw you do it, like, ten times today," said Leandra.

"What are you doing?"

"I'm deleting the pictures of your nephew from your phone," said Leandra. "Assuming Janis only sent those photos to family, Juliet would only be able to get them from someone who received the message. Since we are going to Winter Hill now, it's not unthinkable that she would get the pictures from your phone. So now," she tapped Clear All in the Trash folder, "they're gone."

"That's...really smart," I said. There was silence for a few minutes until I couldn't stand it anymore. "I can't stand the silence."

"Why don't you just say something conversational then?" said Leandra. "What do you want to talk about?"

"What exactly would you have me say to you for conversation?" I asked patiently.

"Well, we are going to a dangerous place that I lived in for two years. I'd probably start asking about that."

"...That's rude."

"So? You're going there; you should know as much about it as you can," said Leandra.

"Still, rude."

"Jesus Christ," said Leandra, "you think I'm going to break down bawling if you mention Winter Hill?"

"Oh, come on! That is not something I'm going to ask someone I don't know that well," I said, exasperated, "and you should be damn skeptical of anyone who starts a conversation like that on their first time meeting you."

"Fine, just don't ask something if you don't want the answer," said Leandra coldly.

I groaned, frustrated, and we sat in silence for a bit. Leandra kept looking down at her tablet, sometimes whispering numbers or words—I couldn't figure out which. It was dark, and I was speeding where I could, but I didn't want the conversation to end on that note.

"How do you know so much about Seeing?" I asked as casually as I could.

"My Mom could See," said Leandra, and I could tell by her voice that she didn't want to talk about it.

"Huh," I said. Silis yawned loudly in the back seat. "Seriously, though. We're going to Winter Hill, and you're still hurt from this morning. Are you...OK with this?"

"They can't do anything to me," said Leandra without looking up. There was something strange about how she said it.

"What about me, or Silis?" I said skeptically.

Leandra looked across at me, and her tablet illuminated her yellow eyes. "You can take 'em."

"OK then," I said, feeling no better about the situation.

"You know what the cult was about, right?" said Leandra.

"Um, crazy mean cult things?" I ventured.

"No. Juliet was famous for being a miracle healer," said Leandra. Silis put his nose in her ear and sniffed. She scratched his neck. "The bad things that happened, they only happened to us."

"Who?" I inquired.

"Her family, who lived there."

"Huh," I said, feeling awkward. "So, no sacrificing goats or anything?"

"No, not that kind of cult," said Leandra.

"Huh. So, how did she heal people?"

"She didn't," Leandra said dryly. "She would find sick people with wealthy relatives and invite them to the house. She made a big show of things. She gave them all this big speech she made up from books in Latin from her dad's old library. All she was really doing was waiting for the person to die. When their soul was about to leave, she'd bring in Bjorn or my mom. They were the only two that could see ghosts. She'd make them watch until they saw the soul leave. She had some way of attracting ghosts to that room."

Leandra looked down at the meteorite fragment again. "I'm pretty sure it was with the meteorites, now. Then she'd sing some song in Latin, and the ghosts in the room would push the soul back into the body for a bit. The dying person would have a moment of 'bliss,' they called it, when the soul sort of lived in the body without recognizing what was wrong with it. They would proclaim what a miracle it was, how great it was, then Juliet would stop singing, and the ghosts would stop, and the person would die 'a beautiful death.'"

Leandra's voice got quiet as she studied the piece of meteorite between her fingers. "Nothing beautiful in it at all. After Mom died, it was just Bjorn, and he wasn't as good at seeing ghosts, so

Juliet tried to get Tori to see ghosts by almost killing her."

"What?" I said, because what she was saying was too horrible to believe.

"Trauma can cause people to see ghosts," Leandra said matter-of-factly. "That's what happened to you, right?"

"Yeah, but," I said slowly, "you can see ghosts..."

Leandra didn't speak for a bit. Then she said, "Juliet never learned that."

In the House of Mothers

"Hey, Grandma!" said Janis as the Mini Coop pulled into the driveway of Darcy's house. Janis hopped over to Grandma Lilly and gave her a hug.

"My dear, don't fret, now," Grandma Lilly said encouragingly to Janis, who was almost in tears.

"I'm so scared, Grandma. It seemed so invasive, so personal, like she was right there, about to take him away from me!" sobbed Janis.

"I know, dear, they can be that way, but you know very well the visions do not always turn out the way you think they will."

"But Grandma, they were looking at his picture and wanted to take him!" Janis said, entering the house with a welcoming gust of warmth.

"I know, dear," said Grandma Lilly calmly. "Let's go greet everyone before there is a fuss."

Darcy and her husband Tobias were still up with Mark and Timmy. Darcy and Tobias's kids, Jasper and Stephanie, had been put to bed, but Grandma Lilly winked at Stephanie, who was watching stealthily from the top of the stairs.

"I wish Mom was here. I wouldn't feel so scared; she always gets me to think clearly about these sorts of things," said Janis in a panic. "Not that you're no help, Gram!" she added hastily. "I'm sorry, I'm just so worried."

"You have every right to be so, dear," said Grandma Lilly, sitting down on the sofa next to Tim. He was sleeping soundly in a blue blanket covered in fish.

Grop sauntered up and put his wrinkled bulldog mutt face in her lap, and she petted him before he went back to sleeping on his bed.

"I'm still confused. What exactly did you See?" asked Darcy, curled up on the couch with a fresh cup of coffee.

"It was so brief," said Janis, "but like I said, it was those pictures I sent all of you of Timmy on the phone, and a woman was holding one, and she said 'Bring him here. He's the one like smoke,' and it felt..." Janis swallowed, "so foul, like she was a witch or some terrible thing. It felt like a nightmare."

"But that wasn't all?" asked Mark attentively.

"No. I saw Yvonne's Trooper outside a gate. It felt like the same place. And someone was climbing up a window, but..." Janis trailed off. "It was strange, like there was something bad up there."

"What does that mean?" asked Darcy.

"I don't know!" sobbed Janis, Mark rubbed her back. "And I don't know if I've sent Yvonne into a trap or made it worse." Janis sank her head into Mark's shoulder.

"We've been in touch with Gerald all evening," said Darcy to Grandma Lilly. "They have a sheriff's deputy accompanying them to Winter Hill."

"He sleeps so soundly, little dove." Grandma Lilly sighed, stroking Timmy's brow, then sat back up quickly. "Well, it's time for me to be off."

"But you just got here," said Janis nervously. "Surely you can stay until we hear from Mom?"

"Janis, I'm sure Grandma wants to go home and sleep in her own bed," said Darcy.

"It's all right, my dove," said Grandma Lilly patiently. "Come with me to the car, will you?"

"It's just so real, Gram," said Janis, leading Grandma Lilly back to the Mini Coop. The lights flashed when she unlocked the car. "I've never had a vision like this before. I'm so scared something bad is going to happen."

"I know, dear. It's nothing to be ashamed of."

"Nobody else gets it except Mom. I've never had a vision that told me something bad before."

"Perhaps it is not bad," said Grandma Lilly thoughtfully. "Perhaps it is showing you something great, and you simply don't know the context yet."

"Oh, I hope so." Janis started to cry again. "I can't bear the thought of something happening to him, or Yva."

"Shush shush shush, dove, go back in and enjoy your time with your siblings and your little one. He's as safe as safe can be," said Grandma Lilly.

"You sure? Have you Seen anything?" Janis asked hopefully.

"Not that you don't already know," said Grandma Lilly, "but I know your mother, I know Gerald, I know Yvonne, and I know you. Whatever foulity will come of your vision will be overcome."

"Does that actually work, or is it something they just tell you in movies?" Janis said while wiping her eyes.

"Always in stories, my pet," Grandma Lilly bopped her on the nose with her finger. "Just remember that you are also in one. Goodnight, my dear."

How much of what we do is believing it will work?

And at the end of the day, who cares?

It's the act that counts, and it's a Chime's job to figure out how to do it best. This can be difficult, because it means you have to face yourself. You have to see what your deepest fear is, then tell it to strangers in the most intimate way, through music.

This is not easy, and sometimes the people you give your gift to help will take it and use it against you.

- Leandra's notes on the Chime, Meadowlark Book of Myths

Winter Hill

Yvonne Meadowlark Rainier

"I'm not saying there's no God," said Leandra. "I'm saying humans have a unique way of turning something pure into something evil. If there is a hell, it won't be anything worse than what we can do on Earth. Only creatures of free will could possibly create so much evil."

"You don't care much for the world, do you?" I said dryly.

"I care a lot for the world." Leandra stared through the Trooper's windshield at the ominous outline of Winter Hill. "I just don't think it cares that much for us."

"You know, we need to talk about your conversation skills," I said, rubbing my temples. "It's usually good policy to say something optimistic or uplifting before doing something scary."

"You need to find out a better coping mechanism than the 'happy thoughts' of a sarcastic cynic," countered Leandra.

"Touché," I conceded.

We were sitting in the Trooper outside the gate of Winter Hill, delaying the inevitable by looking up at the gate, which was an ornate fortification made of wrought iron. Fortunately, someone had left it open, but I didn't feel bold enough to drive through it.

A giant white manor sat at the end of the drive, and it looked exceptionally creepy in the moonlight. It was snowing, and a faint white blanket covered everything, reflecting the moonlight in different directions. It was windy out as well.

There were ghosts milling about everywhere, much the same as they had around the meteorites. As I watched them, however, they appeared to be somewhat more confused and frustrated than the others had been. A few of them had become aware of the meteorite Leandra had and were meandering over to the Trooper.

It is incredibly eerie to see snow fall through ghosts.

"There's not much going on," said Leandra, looking up at the dark house that stood at the end of the grand drive. The advancing ghosts didn't seem to bother her in the slightest. "If Juliet and Lester are here, they'll be in the back of the building where the bedrooms are."

"What about Bjorn?" I asked.

Leandra scratched her chin, and her face was strangely concerned. "Hopefully he's not here at all."

"Right," I said, looking back at Silis. I knew I could count on my faithful hound for protection, but I didn't want him hurt.

And, oh man, nobody wanted to see me mad if my dog got hurt.

"We should walk," said Leandra briskly.

"Walk?" I said, looking at the grounds full of creepy trees, the empty, dark windows, the frost-covered roof tiles, and the ghosts. "This is the frickin' Shining hotel, and you want to just walk on over there?"

Leandra grumbled, "No, I don't, but I think we should." With that, she opened the car door and got out. I noticed she left her backpack behind, but I was sure she had all sorts of things stuffed away in her pockets. Sure enough, when I got outside the Trooper, she had on a black beanie and gloves. The frigid wind multiplied my already existing goose bumps.

"Brrr," I said, grabbing my jacket out of the back seat. Silis had been lying on it, and it was toasty warm. I stopped the dog before he could hop out. "You're going on a leash here, bud." A chilly breeze blew harshly against the car, and I was thankful that Grandma Lilly had warned me to bring a jacket.

"Yeah, no zombie dogs," said Leandra.

"What?" I said. It was hard to hear through the hood of my coat.

"Nothin'."

Silis jumped out of the car, and I looked up at the house. "What this place really needs is a shitload of cats," I said decisively. "Ghosts hate cats."

"You need to sleep," said Leandra.

"Fact," I said, closing the driver's-side door and making sure all the doors got locked. "But highly irrelevant."

"Let's go this way." Leandra started off into the dark of the trees skirting the mansion. I tried not to run too quickly after her as I felt the creepy dread of being alone at night with a bunch of sauntering ghosts shimmering around me.

Our shoes crunched over branches as I followed Leandra's silhouette through the thickets. Fortunately, there was some sort of light on in the backyard, which reassured me that we weren't walking farther into the forest.

I heard Leandra's boots hit something solid, and soon Silis's feet were clicking on stone. Underneath a dusting of snow, I felt brick.

"Careful, it's slick," said Leandra. "It's an old path to the river."

"Where's the river?" I asked wearily.

"Far away," said Leandra. "You would hear it if we were close."

The path of bricks led us out of the forest into an expansive courtyard. The light I had been following was a buzzing lamp over an old, dilapidated greenhouse. The old glass door was broken, as was part of the roof. It looked much older than the rest of the architecture. There was also a burned-out structure next to it.

"What's that?" I asked with alarm, staring at the rickety, blackened planks.

Leandra looked over at it stiffly, then turned away. Without stopping, she said, "The garden shed."

"What happened to it?" I asked, pulling Silis away from sniffing it.

"I burned it down," Leandra said evenly.

"You?" I said. "Uh, OK."

We rounded the courtyard, and I saw the looming structure of the mansion pan out over the yard. Leandra was scanning the windows, searching for something I could not see.

Bjorn was shaking, and not just because the cold air from the open window was hitting him. His sweatshirt was not keeping him warm anymore because it was drenched in sweat. He tried to open up his cellphone, but his hands wouldn't work right.

Lester was dead. Bjorn knew he was dead. He had stopped breathing and wasn't moving. He couldn't see the ghosts, couldn't do the ritual the way Antigone had. Bjorn's hands shook as he crouched on the window ledge. His brother was dead because of him.

Leandra stopped abruptly, looking in alarm at a top-story window. "Shit, try to distract him!" she said firmly, and ran toward the house.

"Oh shit," I hissed as I saw Bjorn sitting on the sill of one of the fourth-story windows. A faint light was glowing behind him. He was shaking, and it was clear that he was in distress. Silis whined.

"Oh, hey! Bjorn!" I said in a reassuring but happy voice. I don't think he could hear me. Leandra was climbing up the window moldings.

I ran closer to the house. "Bjorn!"

Silis barked.

Bjorn seemed to realize we were there and stared at us. I was afraid he was going to slip off the sill, but he caught himself.

"Hey, hi!" I said, "I'm Yvonne. I, uh, saw you earlier. How are you doing?"

"Go away!" shouted Bjorn, but Silis's barking seemed to keep him planted on the sill. Leandra was climbing up the third-story balcony, and I wanted to scream at her to get down.

"We're not here to bother you," I said, trying to figure out what would be helpful to say. "I just want to talk to you, all right? What's going on? Why are you on the sill?"

Bjorn's hands were shaking violently as he wiped his nose. "None of your concern," he said gravely, and I could barely hear him.

"It looks warmer inside," I said. "Why don't you lean backward? Aren't you cold?"

"I don't care," stuttered Bjorn, "I don't care about the—"

Bjorn yelled as Leandra leapt through the window and pushed him back into the room.

"Jeez!" I shouted. "Leandra!"

"We're good!" I heard faintly over the wind. "Stay down there!"

Leandra pulled Bjorn farther away from the window. Bjorn offered little resistance, as he was barely able to move. His skin was cold, and his face was pale. Leandra spotted Lester's still body lying on the bed.

"Oh, for fuck's sake," said Leandra, running to the bed. She inspected the empty glass in Lester's hands and swore.

"He's dead," sobbed Bjorn. "He's dead because I can't see the ghosts."

"There are no ghosts in here in to see," said Leandra angrily, pulling her glove off to feel for a vein in Lester's wrist. "Did you check his pulse?"

Bjorn shook his head. Leandra couldn't tell if she felt something or not. She smashed a mirror hanging on the wall with her elbow and put one of the smaller shards near his mouth. It fogged ever so slightly.

"Did she use the same flask?" Leandra asked urgently. "The gold and red one?"

"Yeah," said Bjorn quietly, and Leandra snatched the small flask from the pedestal and took it over to the fire to inspect.

"Did she change it? Or was it the same stuff as last time?" asked Leandra insistently.

"What?" asked Bjorn, rather confused.

Leandra put a drop of the flask's contents on her finger and tasted it. She spit it into the fire immediately and tossed the flask in after it. She looked stiffly back at Lester. Then she pulled the curtains off the window and tossed one over him.

"Tori drank it and lived," said Bjorn hopefully.

Leandra took a red blanket from a chair and put it over Bjorn's legs, which were still shaking. "Tori drank cough syrup."

Bjorn stared at her blankly. Leandra gestured with her head, as if to say, "Don't believe me?" and knelt down and reached under the bed. From under a spring in the mattress, she pulled out an old cardboard cough syrup package, slightly moth-eaten. She held it up for Bjorn to see. "I switched hers."

Bjorn's shoulders trembled, and he looked at his brother and then back at Leandra. "He's really dying?"

"If he drank Juliet's witch shit, he needs a hospital now," Leandra said evasively.

Bjorn looked down at his chest, almost laughing, "I think I'm dying too."

"Did you spit it out?" asked Leandra, inspecting Bjorn's complexion.

"Yeah," said Bjorn.

Leandra bit her cheek. "You'll be fine if you keep warm and wait for the ambulance." She touched his forehead with her thumb. "I think you've got hypothermia big time though."

"Ambulance?" whispered Bjorn, and he shook his head with disbelief. "Ambulances don't come here."

"They will if I call them," said Leandra. "I can't imagine anyone tried to sell all that radio equipment they had stashed up there. I can get an ambulance here."

"But the ghosts." Bjorn's cold hand grabbed Leandra's arm weakly. "The ghosts—"

"There are no ghosts in here," said Leandra, a little more patiently. She looked around the room again to be sure. "Bjorn, even if there were, that wouldn't have saved them. Any of them."

Leandra pushed Bjorn's hand off her arm. He groaned, as the movement hurt.

"Did you ingest any of it?" asked Leandra.

"A little," croaked Bjorn. "You sure you can get an ambulance here?"

"Eventually," said Leandra, "There could be one here anywhere from now till a few hours from now. But one is going to come. Dad's on his way too; he can help you."

Bjorn scowled. "He won't help me."

"Yeah, he will," said Leandra.

Bjorn gave her a dagger look, but it was not so effective with him shivering so violently, "Leandra..." His voice trailed away, "I don't want it to end like this. I never got to tell her I was sorry."

"Tori's fine, Bjorn," said Leandra. "She's been safe this whole time."

"How do you know?" he half sobbed, half laughed. "How could you know where she is? Did one of them tell you?"

"No," said Leandra.

"Then how?" demanded Bjorn.

Leandra's lips tightened, and she shrugged. "I just know."

"How?" Bjorn gritted his teeth, and Leandra saw the old hurt, the abandonment, all the things he suffered silently through the years. She had seen the look on her own face in the mirror. It was a dense, terrifying emotion. Rage could not contain it, nor pity. Just a hollow questions she had eventually found the answer to herself.

Leandra didn't say anything, just pulled Bjorn closer to the fire. She picked up some old magazines from the floor. She ripped them apart, crumpled them up, and tossed them on the dying flames. The paper burned quickly and created bursts of high heat. She put a stack of the magazines next to Bjorn, then she put some larger logs onto the fire. Suddenly, she said, "You didn't hurt Justinia."

Bjorn looked up in shock. "What?"

Leandra looked at him sideways. "The rape conviction against you. It was wrong." She pulled off her beanie and stuck it on Bjorn's head. "It wasn't you. Justinia lied because she was afraid of Lester."

Bjorn bit his knuckles. His shoulders shook.

Leandra grabbed the cardboard package for the cough syrup and threw it in the fire. It burned quickly and gave off a bright burst of light. Bjorn's shoulders still hadn't stopped trembling. "All of them, Bjorn; they all used you as the scapegoat. Including me."

Bjorn licked his dry lips and said quietly, "How could you know what happened?"

"Remember, I was there?" said Leandra. "It was just after my mom died. I was down by the river when I heard Justinia crying. I came up behind the shed and banged on the wall. I must have given Justinia a chance to escape, because when I came around the other side, she was there with her dress ripped, crying and trying to break free of your arms." Leandra scratched the back of her head. "I got so angry, I just remember red. But it was Lester; he was still in the shed. You broke the door open, and she ran. They blamed you, because they were afraid of Lester."

Bjorn didn't say anything.

"I remember pulling Justinia back into her room. She wouldn't stop crying. I don't know how Juliet covered it up. Justinia wanted to leave. I didn't want her to go; she was the only other girl there my age. I burned down the shed. Tori told me later that she'd seen Lester take Justinia into the shed. It wasn't you." Leandra shrugged, and in the firelight, it was hard to tell if the shine on her cheeks was tears or sweat. "Even though she told me, I blamed you, unfairly. In my mind, all of you were guilty. At that time, it didn't matter whose fault it was. It was all wrong. I'm sorry, Bjorn. I was so worried about Tori and I—I should have seen...they were worse to you." Leandra ran her fingers through her hair. "At least Justinia got out."

Bjorn laughed, which surprised them both. "You got her out." He shook his head. "The only time I saw Juliet get shaken was when Tori came up to her and asked why you'd kissed Justinia." Bjorn shook his head again. "All that, but the thought of you kissing a girl made Juliet insane." Bjorn paused a bit. "I didn't see you for weeks."

Leandra shrugged. "Whatever."

Bjorn and Leandra both knew what had happened, but while Bjorn was trapped in the past, Leandra was all too aware of the present. She peered at Lester, lying still on the bed. She hardly felt a pulse when she checked. She knew there was nothing they could do for him, but part of her wanted to help him, though another part of her wanted the opposite. Leandra fell back on logic. "We can't do anything for him," she said.

She saw a flash of light on the ceiling and went to the window. Yvonne was waving the light from her flashlight up at the window, trying to figure out what had happened. Silis was dancing about her feet in angst. Leandra gave her a thumbs-up and signaled for her to go through the door. "I'll meet you there," Leandra shouted.

Yvonne looked less than thrilled, but went inside with Silis.

Leandra closed the window to keep some of the warmth in. She turned to Bjorn. "Where's Juliet?"

"Downstairs," he whispered, as if they might suddenly be heard.

Leandra nodded. She looked around inquisitively until her eyes settled on the pedestal. She lifted the heavy object with some difficulty and tipped it over in front of the door so it could only open enough for her to squeeze through. "When I leave, push this in front of the door. The fire department can break it down," she said.

Bjorn nodded in appreciation. He looked over at the revolver on the floor. Leandra looked at it and back at him. "You all right?"

Bjorn nodded several times. "Yeah."

"All right. Don't let the fire go out." Leandra closed the door, and her voice sounded muffled through the planks. "Push the pedestal over here."

Bjorn pushed it in front of the door with his feet. Leandra tried to open the door, but it was difficult even for her. Frail little Juliet would not be getting in. "You're good, Bjorn. I'm going to find the radio, but even if I don't get to it, help's on the way." Leandra didn't wait for a reply. She turned down the hall, her flashlight illuminating the eerily familiar hallways.

Bjorn nodded at the door, and tears fell down his face. He didn't know if it was relief, joy, or anguish that caused them. At the moment, he didn't care; he was convinced that the pedestal wasn't enough to keep his mother from him, and he jerked in alarm at every sound in the hallway. Slowly, his eyes found the revolver that was sitting stoically on the floor. He gulped and turned away, pulling the blanket farther around himself. Whatever was going to happen, he had no choice but to wait.

The study with the radio was at the other end of the building. When Leandra had watched Kubrick's The Shining for the first time, the room with the radio had reminded her completely of Winter Hill, and she'd had to turn the movie off. When she had finished watching it later, she'd stayed up all night studying for her HAM license test so she could use the radio legally if she was ever stuck in a snowed-in ski lodge.

Or Winter Hill.

Leandra found the familiarity of the house disturbing. Everything was the same, except vacant, dark, and dusty. She opened the study door carefully. She tried the light switch with no luck. She moved quickly to the old radio on the desk, shoving books and papers onto the floor. After a few minutes of tinkering, she got the generator next to it roaring.

Soon the radio was on and tuned to the sheriff stations. The higher bands the Sheriff's Department ran its radio on were usually off limits to civilian communication, but she was more than certain there was illegal equipment for monitoring the radio. She had also memorized the frequencies for the area. She'd have to tell Beatrice that her paranoia had paid off for once.

Then she remembered that she would not be able to.

Shut up, Leandra, she told herself sternly, and work.

Leandra sent out a call and listened to the static of the station. An unintelligible message came through, but someone was definitely listening.

"Roger, I repeat, an ambulance is needed at Winter Hill—"

"Leandra?" said a small voice behind her.

Leandra spun around and shouted, "Tori?" though she had hardly finished before something hard hit her neck. It was enough to knock her into the generator, and she was out before she could see the radio get smashed with a silver candlestick.

Juliet stepped into the light of Leandra's flashlight lying next to her. In her bony hands was a voice recorder that still contained a recording of Tori's voice from long ago. Juliet had played it constantly for the last eight years.

"Leandra? Where's Leandra? I want Leandra!" Tori's voice echoed.

"She's right here," whispered Juliet, and hordes of ghosts swarmed around her and bent over Leandra with concern. They scattered when Juliet came nearer.

How much of an animal's ability to survive is not based on its place in the food chain, but its will to fight against it?

- Note scribbled by Gerald Meadowlark, Meadowlark Book of Myths

THE GREENHOUSE

Leandra Meadowlark, Winter Hill, Eight Years Prior

The sound of scraping jeans.

Scrich scrich scrich scrich.

I woke up immediately, knowing what had happened before I saw the door close.

Tori was gone.

Ba-dump, ba-dump, ba-dump.

My heart was slamming against my chest. If I was discovered...

Badumpbadumpbadumpbadump.

"Tori!" I whispered, pushing the door open. Tori was lying on a red bed in her nightdress.

Bjorn stood up from a stool beside the bed, shock and anger on his face. "What are you doing here?" he asked.

I acted scared.

Bjorn looked at Tori, then quickly back at me, then tried to push me back out into the hall. I hit him in the stomach and then across the neck with a hardback book. Bjorn collapsed.

Tori was barely breathing. The glass in her limp hand was empty. Her body was cold.

I tasted from the glass; cough syrup. Better than poison, but it was prescription strength and still enough to kill her. It was all I'd been able to find that appeared similar enough to the poison to be mistaken for it.

Tori was going to die.

I took Bjorn's cellphone and coat.

Ghosts were all around us, looking afraid. They knew Tori was dying.

"Help me," I implored them. "Help me get her out of here."

I took the blankets from the bed and tied her to my back, and then I climbed out the window. My fingers held fast to the molding as I carefully lowered us both to the ground. I was so glad I was wearing the pair of jeans I'd stolen under my dress. Ghosts surrounded us, trying to help somehow. We made it to the bottom. I ran. The ghosts could not follow.

The geese hissed as I ran past them with Tori on my back. I ran as quickly as I could. I had to get to the road, flag down a car, and get them to take Tori to a hospital.

The glare of flashlights found us. I panicked and ran to the only safe place I saw; the old greenhouse.

I set Tori down and locked the old iron-framed door behind me. I could not see through the old panes of glass, ornately framed by intricate ironwork. I pulled over a metal shelf to barricade the door. They would have to break their precious antique greenhouse to get inside.

I picked up a shovel, scissors, a rake, a stake, everything that could be used to stab someone, and placed them near Tori and me. I pulled sacks of fertilizer around us like a bunker and pulled her into my lap. She was so cold.

My heart beat loudly.

Badump, badump, badump.

I pulled out Bjorn's cellphone and called the police.

"911, what is your emergency?"

"I need an ambulance, cops, and someone who will do something about a bunch of murders at Winter Hill, NOW."

"What has happened?"

"My cousin's been poisoned. We're locked in the greenhouse, but they'll find us soon. Please send someone out quickly! She's freezing to death."

"We're sending a patrol car out now. What's your name?"

"I don't need a patrol car; I need a goddamn ambulance!"

"Is this Leandra Meadowlark?"

"Goddamnit, send out a goddamn ambulance! My cousin's dying!"

"There's no need to swear, young lady. Just let us know where you are and we'll get to you soon."

I swore loudly and clicked the phone closed. Tori began to shiver uncontrollably in my lap. I pulled off Bjorn's coat and put it over her. "It's going to be OK, Tori. They're sending an ambulance."

She didn't respond.

"Tori, Tori, stay with me, stay awake!"

"Cold." She shivered. "Why?"

"I don't know, babe. Don't worry, we're going to get you safe."

But I knew that wasn't true. I started rocking her back and forth in my lap, wondering what I could do. The men were probably hearing about my call through dispatch on their giant radio in the house right now. We were dead.

"Goddamn it, goddamn it," I chanted as I rocked us back and forth.

I pulled up the phone; ten minutes of battery left. Who could I possibly call?

I scrolled throughout the contacts; no one I wanted to talk to. I didn't know Dad's phone number; they were relentless at hiding that from me.

I found Twitter. Bjorn was logged into the Winter Hill feed. Would it do anything? It was worth a shot.

I typed slowly, with cold fingers.

SEND AMBULANCE 2 WINTER HILL GREENHOUSE.

I copied and pasted it over and over. If we didn't live, at least these fuckers would have to deal with a wall of obnoxious tweets.

"Hey Ruby," said Deputy Martinez into his cellphone.

"Hey Roland, you need to do me a favor and get up and check out Winter Hill. My daughter says there's some big thing going on on Twitter about it. Might be an out-of-control party or something."

"What are they saying?" asked Martinez.

"To send an ambulance to the greenhouse."

"So why are you sending me?"

"It's the Harrows' place. Technically, we can't go there."

"Is that why you're technically sending me on a call on my personal cellphone?"

"Technically, they fund the entire county Sheriff's Department."

"But I'm the rookie deputy that can get away with a polite inquiry?"

"You got it."

"Any history there?"

"It's creepy as hell."

"OK, I'm off," said Martinez, turning back out onto the highway. "Give me the details."

"Where is Tori?" hissed Juliet. "Where did that little bitch take her?"

"I don't think Bjorn's neck looks good," Lester said dryly, inspecting the bruise there. Bjorn was still unconscious.

"They are at the greenhouse," said Bastion, calling from the radio room balcony above. "She called the sheriff."

"Where's his phone, did she take it?" Juliet said harshly.

Then the doorbell rang, and Juliet composed herself poisedly.

"You don't need an ambulance?" confirmed Deputy Martinez.

"No, deputy, we are just fine," said Juliet politely.

"Where is your greenhouse located? I'd like to take a look, if you don't mind."

"I'm afraid you'll need a search warrant for that."

"Is Leandra Meadowlark here?"

"Le-who?" asked Juliet, flustered.

"Leandra Meadowlark, is she here?"

"Ah, no, she went to bed. Poor girl is of a sickly disposition. You can come back and see her in the morning," Juliet prompted. "I insist."

Martinez looked inside the house. Everything looked in place.

"What's your name again?" asked Juliet.

"Deputy Martinez."

"Oh yes," Juliet smiled far too sweetly. "Let me get your badge number, and I'll be sure to call in and tell your superiors what a thorough job you have done."

"I'm sure you will. Mind if I come in?"

"No, you can wait right there." Juliet, still smiling sweetly, waved Lester over for a pen and paper.

I put my coat over Tori and buried her as carefully into the fertilizer bags as I could. I was climbing the greenhouse shelves, trying to get to the roof.

Shit, shit, he's leaving! I grabbed the small shovel and began pounding on the new plastic roof with all my might; the ice-covered plastic cracked. A few adrenaline-fueled hits cracked it enough to look through.

Is that a cop car? Holy shit, that's a cop car!

"Thank you, Deputy Martinez," said Juliet, holding her hand out like a tray. "I'm sure you can find your way home from here."

Martinez gave the mansion one last look and nodded before walking back down the drive to his patrol car.

Martinez opened his patrol car door and looked back at the grounds. He knew it was unlikely he'd hear the end of this tomorrow. He knew some of the rumors about the Harrow mansion and how it was best to stay the fuck away from it because of money, politics, blah blah blah...

But Martinez could tell something was wrong.

A dog started barking, and people started talking in among the trees, and Martinez heard someone yelling. Two men standing by the gate made it clear by their presence that it was time for him to leave. Something was wrong, but he knew there was little he could do alone, if the rumors about Winter Hill were true.

Martinez wasn't an idiot. He got into his patrol car, turned on the heater, and drove down the gravel drive.

I hit the roof with all my might and got it to split farther. I stood on one of the shelves and, with effort, pulled the roofing material apart. I saw the patrol car driving away.

"HEEELLLP! HEEEEY! I NEED AN AMBULANCE! FUCK! COME BACK! HEEEELP!!!" I screamed.

A bullet hit the roof near me. I flinched and fell back, off the shelf, and landed hard on the ground. I screamed as my hand erupted in pain and almost immediately began to swell. I was sure it was broken.

"Just come out, Leandra," said Spail, one of the longtime devotees, from outside. "No one's coming to save you."

I scrambled back to Tori and pulled her against my side, grabbing the shovel with my good hand.

"Stay the fuck away from us!" I yelled, trembling from fear, pain, and cold. I had done what I could and failed; I didn't expect to live to see the dawn. I really wanted to live—more than anything, I wanted to live—but if the sheriff's deputy was gone, I didn't want to live the life that would be impending if I survived.

"That's quite enough, child," said Juliet, her snow boots clomping up the steps. The door rattled violently as she tried to open it.

"We can bring this greenhouse down on both of you, and you can look forward to a very lonely future, or you can come out and we can talk," said Juliet coldly.

"Talk about what?" I cried. "How you'll kill Tori for your fucking magic tricks?"

"See, that is what you don't understand," said Juliet, circling the glass walls to where my voice was coming from. Her silhouette reflected strangely through the old glass panes, and she looked like the monster I knew she was. "Tori has a special gift, and tonight, it was going to be amplified. That might still be possible if you let us in."

"So you can kill her, like you killed my mother?" I pulled Tori closer.

"Oh, you simple child," said Juliet impatiently, stopping right in front of us on the other side of the glass. I was trembling so bad that the shovel shook in my hand and my teeth rattled in my skull. It was so cold. "Your mother's death was tragic. Tori is different. You wouldn't want to put yourself above the rest of your family, would you? We do not tolerate such behavior in our family."

I heard the click of gun hammers being cocked and squeezed my eyes shut.

"What Tori will become tonight is more important than any of us, including you." Juliet said it sweetly, as if to make the statement less horrific. "You wouldn't be the first to die in the line of protecting another from what you don't understand. Poor child, you are so confused."

"I'm not confused," I spat. "This is evil."

"Silence!" commanded Juliet.

"SHUT UP, YOU FUCKING MONSTER!"

"Tsk, tsk, we're going to have to do something about those words you love so much," Juliet said in a singsong voice.

"Tori is dying!"

"No, she is transforming," said Juliet. "If you could calm your unstable mind, you might be able to understand that."

"SHE'S DYING!" I shouted. "You fucking twat, Juliet! I was there when my mother died; I know what death looks like. Is this what you want? Is this what you're about? I hope you die like this, Juliet, ALONE AND AFRAID!" I shouted.

Juliet sighed. "My dear, I think that is what is actually going to happen to you."

I sobbed quietly and wondered what the fuck I had done to deserve this. Good God, just let me die, let this be over. There was talking outside as they coordinated how to get in without breaking the glass on top of Tori.

Tori began breathing erratically. I held her forehead and kissed it.

"I'm sorry, I'm sorry, I'm so sorry," I sobbed before letting her go. I knew it was the last time I would be let near her. One way or another, they would never let me see her again. I picked up the shovel and stood facing the door. I'd take a few of them with me, at least. Or they would shoot me. Either way was better than what they wanted. I wondered if Tori would remember me, or if they'd pretend I didn't exist, like Justinia.

"If it won't come open, shoot it," said Juliet.

I stifled a sob.

The door rumbled with the impact of someone trying one last time to dismantle the doorframe. I dropped the shovel. My hand was shaking too much. I couldn't do it. They would take me away easily, back to a white room with a white dress and no books except their cult rhetoric. Juliet would pay her way through lawyers and policemen to make sure I could never return to my dad. Eventually, she would kill me somehow, but not before having me give birth to a few children she could raise and do the same thing to that she was doing to Tori.

I'd be completely alone.

I saw a piece of broken plastic from the roof. I latched onto it with trembling hands and tested it on my finger; it was razor sharp, enough to cut down my wrist, enough to end it. I had read about it in books; they could not undo it. You die quietly from bleeding out, peacefully. It would be my choice, my end. I couldn't describe my relief.

I took a deep breath and prepared myself for death. They would not take me from here alive. Death was better than what they had planned for me, and Dad would Chime for me.

"*Daddy*," I sobbed, holding the plastic below my broken hand. I had promised him I'd be OK. I had lied, and I couldn't even save Tori. *"I'm sorry."*

"Hands up, drop the weapon!" someone shouted behind the greenhouse, and I collapsed. Everywhere, there were people shouting. I covered my head. Several shots were fired, and more shouting happened; dogs barked; I saw flashing red and blue lights. My heart was pounding so hard it didn't register that someone was shouting through the door.

"This is Deputy Martinez. Leandra, are you in there? Leandra Meadowlark!"

"Yes!" I sobbed. "Yes!"

"I got an ambulance coming. Hang on."

"The fuck did you just say?" I said, not believing it.

"There's an ambulance and a shitload of FBI and SWAT on their way," Martinez said. "Hang tight. We'll get you out of there."

I probably should have said something like "'Bout damn time!" or "You're a fucking saint,

Martinez!" but I didn't. I fell on my back and cried like a little girl, and I didn't care who heard me.

It never occurred to my younger self that most people my age didn't know what it felt like to want to die. Not die because you wanted to die, but because you knew what was waiting at the end of the day was worse.

I was living that day all over again, but there was no glass between Juliet and me this time.

As Juliet dragged my semiconscious body closer to the staircase, I remembered the fear and helplessness of that day to the point where my heart rattled in my chest, but I was also quite satisfied that I was much heavier than she remembered.

I saw the faces of ghosts looking down at me, grey and tired. I wasn't sure if they recognized me. Juliet pushed me, and I don't know if the grey I saw pass before my eyes was someone else's ghost or my own.

What parts of themselves are lost, pursuing the completion of a bottomless dam?

What madness do they find there and bring back for the world to see?

- Meadowlark Book of Myths

The Light of Letters

Yvonne Meadowlark Rainier

Fortunately, the back door was unlocked, but the inside of the house was a frickin' maze.

Silis and I were back in the dark kitchen after trying every door. All the doors to the big room were locked. My flashlight was creating creepy shadows across old pots and pans. Most, disgustingly enough, had not been washed in years.

I swore and looked around for some answer and shrieked when I saw a ghost. The black-and-white roller-skating ghost stood in the corner. Silis barked for my benefit, but he immediately went up to sniff her happily. As I took several breaths and tried to get my heart to slow down, she held out her grey hand for Silis to sniff. Silis put his nose right through her ghost hand and seemed to think it immensely entertaining.

"Hey," I said angrily, "that was extremely uncool!"

The roller-skating ghost shrugged apologetically, as if to say, "I can't help that I'm a ghost in a creepy dark house."

"Sorry," I said after a moment. "Can you help us get up there?" I pointed up.

The ghost nodded quickly and waved for us to follow her. The only problem was, she vanished through the stove.

"Um, hey! We can't get through that way!" I called after her.

The ghost's head appeared through the stove, and she waved us on more fervently. I sighed in frustration and went to the stove. I pulled open the door angrily to prove my point, and the entire wall moved back. I shouted in surprise and fell backward. Silis sniffed my face to make sure I was OK. The girl skated through the opening and waved for me to come on.

"Secret passages." I got up shakily. "Of course there would be secret passages. OK, ghost, lead on!"

The roller-skating ghost smiled and walked up a small wooden staircase. She stepped sideways to keep her skates from slipping off the edges of the steps. Silis and I followed, because what else could we do?

We ascended two flights of stairs, and then she led Silis and me through a small wooden door that turned out to be a large painting. "Of course they'd have a creepy secret passageway hidden behind a giant painting," I told Silis quietly.

I hated the Harrows, but I was impressed by their choice in architecture. Our guide skated quickly down the wide hallway. Silis and I ran after her. She stopped in front of a white door and looked back at us worriedly. She nodded to the door.

I looked down at Silis. "Okey dokey then," I said. I opened the door and flooded the space with the light from my super-bright flashlight.

There was a bed, stripped of everything but the mattress, a single open window with billowing white curtains, several empty bookcases, and a ghost sitting on top of the mattress, looking down at the fabric as if she couldn't find what should be there.

I looked back at my ghost guide, and she nodded to the ghost on the bed.

"Uh, hello?" I said, and the grey ghost looked up at me slowly. Then she got up quickly and was suddenly in my face, studying me. I felt a cold hand brush my face as her grey fingers slid over my cheek. At last her expression turned to one of disappointment, and she glided sadly back to the bed.

"She looks like...Leandra," I said to the roller-skating ghost. "Is that...Antigone?"

At the sound of her name, Antigone raised her head again, her many strands of hair flowing through the air like the curtains across the window.

"She's stuck here, she's stuck in the room!" I said. The roller-skating ghost smiled and nodded.

"Oh," I said, clearing my throat. "I see." It was time for me to do ghost work. "Um," I paused and turned back to the roller-skating ghost. "Shouldn't I wait for Leandra?"

The roller-skating ghost shook her head urgently and nodded to Antigone encouragingly.

"OK," I said, and more quietly, I confessed, "probably better this way."

I stepped cautiously toward the bed. "Antigone?"

Antigone's ghost turned slowly to look at me. I could really see her resemblance to Leandra.

I cleared my throat again, finding it more than a little awkward and sad that I was about to evict my dead aunt from the room she had died in.

"Antigone Harrow," I began. Antigone started to look away. "Antigone Meadowlark?"

Antigone turned back and smiled slightly. I had her attention.

"My name is Yvonne Rainier, and this is no longer your home." I said it with as much authority as I could muster. "It's time for you to go."

Antigone inspected me vaguely.

I cleared my throat. "Immediately."

I'd like to claim that Antigone's sudden animation was due to my great abilities at ghost working, but it was more likely due to the shouting we heard that sounded a lot like Leandra.

Antigone fixed her gaze on the door. The roller-skating ghost grabbed Antigone's hand and pulled her out of the room. They both ran right through me, which was totally skin-crawlingly creepy. Silis and I ran after them before the secret painting door closed.

The only recorded time a Chime has ever used his skill to manipulate the dead happened in Mississippi, in 1815.

A boat carrying a Sunday school party flipped, and all the company drowned.

A hermit lived on an island in the river where the boat sank. With his voice, he convinced the ghosts of the drowned to flip the boats of all who neared his island. His ghoulish chanting also mesmerized the alligators to do his bidding, and it wasn't long before the town ordered him burned as a witch, but all attempts to reach his island ended in screams and death.

More than one sensible man swore they saw the drenched forms of women standing on the water, waiting for them to approach. All the while, they could hear the man singing.

The town abandoned the river and stayed clear of the island. Anyone seen leaving the island was shot. For years, for generations, the singing never stopped.

A few years ago, the village decided to try again. The townsfolk took scores of boats and weapons. They reached the island on the brightest day, bribing the gators with freshly slaughtered deer, each boat accompanied and blessed by a priest who uttered scripture and held a cross. It is even rumored that they splashed the bottoms of the boats with holy water.

The only one who volunteered to search the island was a boy. Upon returning, he claimed he had found a small hut in which there was a man, impossibly aged, eyes white with blindness, mouth long void of teeth. He mumbled songs no one knew, surrounded by the vestiges of many white ghosts.

The boy told me himself, "They want ta go, the ghosts."

I leave with this boy in a small boat now, to visit this island in hopes that the Chime will end the haunting of the island for good.

- The final, unfinished entry of the diary of Jenkins Meadowlark, found in the Meadowlark Book of Myths

ANTIGONE

Leandra Meadowlark

I woke up with a familiar feeling of low blood pressure and exposure.

My ankle was sprained, and my jacket was gone. I felt like I had just fallen out of a blender. Many grey ghosts were leaning over me with looks of relief that I had woken up. Judging from my current position at the bottom of the stairs, I ventured to guess that they were the only reason I hadn't joined them.

Juliet was fussing with something by the fireplace, doing some creepy thing she had probably made up.

While she was occupied, I looked up at the balcony. Yvonne was still around somewhere with Silis, and the radio had made contact with someone. Help would arrive soon.

I tried to move and felt pain in all different parts of my body. I looked up at the marble floor of the great hall and back up the tall staircase that led to the radio room four flights above.

"Did you push me down the stairs?" I asked incredulously. "Three...three times?"

Juliet didn't respond.

I laughed into my arm and sat up stiffly. The ribs I had injured earlier hurt the most. My elbows and legs felt bumped and bruised to pieces. I moved my neck around gingerly, knowing that was what was most vulnerable to severe injury. I saw Juliet's revolver on the table. "Didn't have it in you to finish it?"

"I want to know only one thing," said Juliet quietly. "Where is my daughter?"

"She's safe," I said, wiping my nose. My hand shook. I couldn't quite move my leg right. "'The fuck else do you want from her?"

"That's not what I asked," hissed Juliet. She didn't turn around, as if she didn't want to look at me.

Suddenly the ghosts all turned to me as if I was a piece of bait on a lure, and their bodies swarmed me.

I'm not quite sure what happened, but with the onslaught of souls pushing against me, I felt a sickeningly disorienting sensation of emotions, struggles, fear, confusion, and loss. It ended abruptly. When I opened my eyes, the ghosts looked confused and alarmed. One tried to touch my shoulder with concern. A few mouthed down at me, "I'm sorry."

They looked at me imploringly. I smiled at them. "'S OK."

"Your ramblings are not clear, my dear," said Juliet, misinterpreting my meaning entirely. The ghosts made way for her, but they looked at her with disdain. Juliet's eyes looked dark, and none of the chemicals she'd used or makeup she wore could disguise her ugly soul. Her voice was low and gravelly. "I did not hear you say a location."

"No, you didn't," I said tiredly, "and I wouldn't tell you if I knew."

"You will tell me, child," whispered Juliet. "You will tell me."

The ghosts swarmed me again. I closed my eyes and counted breaths as the storms of chaos radiated in my brain. It was extremely unpleasant, but I knew it wouldn't kill me. I counted breaths and found a rhythm in my heartbeat.

Ba-dump, ba-dump.

I clicked my teeth along with it too.

Ba-dump click click ti ta tick tick, ba-dump click click ti ta tick tick.

The swarm of chaos vanished, and I opened my eyes again. The ghosts were terrified, trying to put themselves between Juliet and me. She must not be able to see them very well; it was clear whose side they were on. I tapped my foot to try to get feeling in it again.

"Leave them alone!" I shouted. "What are you doing?"

"You don't know?" said Juliet softly. She tutted. "Of course not; you could not possibly know."

"I don't care what your crazy change-the-world shit plan is. Leave these people alone!"

"They are not people," spat Juliet, "not anymore. This is not harming them."

"I am not going to argue with your crazy." I coughed, and my throat stung from bile. Whatever the ghosts had done felt wrong. Disgustingly wrong.

"She was nothing like you," whispered Juliet, "She was perfect." A tear rolled down her stoic face.

"She is," I agreed, shifting my weight slightly. I continued to tap my feet together. "You know, Juliet, you always loved to point out the things that made me different. The things that you thought made me strange. Maybe it never occurred to you that the things that make me different are what make me great."

"Oh yes," whispered Juliet, "the Chime. A profession for vagabonds."

"Is that why you do it?" I said, grinning darkly.

Juliet's mouth twitched. "I don't know what you mean, poor child. Only men can wield the Chime."

"Whatever," I said, "that's not true at all. You just only saw men recorded in the book of myth as Chimes."

"Foolish—" Juliet began.

"Shut up, Juliet," I said, twisting my body to sit upright. "You think you fooled everyone with your Latin verses? Your hypothetical scripture and hypocritical rhetoric? You were singing to the ghosts, telling them to keep the spirits of the dying in their bodies." I laughed, but it hurt. "All you were doing was manipulating the Chime, like Egor and Byron Meadowlark."

Juliet's expression darkened. She turned to the fireplace. "You don't know that story, Leandra."

"Sure I do," I said.

"There is only one copy of that record, and I have it." Juliet pulled a small black book from her shirt. "You do not know that story."

"Sure I do," I repeated, and I pointed like the sarcastic little shit I am. "That's the story of Egor and Byron Meadowlark and the first attempt at something like Winter Hill." I shrugged. "Didn't turn out that great for them either."

"How—"

"I stole it," I said loudly. "You had one book with you at all times that you wouldn't let anybody read, especially Mom. Of course I stole it. Snuck it from your lock box after you passed out from who knows what the first fuckin' month I had to stay here."

"No," denied Juliet.

"Oh yeah," I said. "The best part is that I took pictures of every page with my iPod. Studied those pages up right good. Course, you broke it with a hammer when you heard me listening to Zappa, but the cloud," I laughed sardonically and whispered mockingly, "it's the future."

Juliet fumed, and I couldn't tell if the crackling sounds I heard were from the fireplace or her brain cells popping.

"You always said I was a delinquent; I was just fulfilling your expectations," I explained.

"I did it better," Juliet seethed. "I changed what they did wrong."

"Yeah, you justify the terrible thing you did by comparing it to something worse. Bravo."

I looked around at all the ghosts. They were calmer now, swaying slightly. Their frustration and fear had turned to a calm sadness. "I mean, I know you can't see the ghosts very well, Juliet, but it doesn't take a strong pair of eyes to see you are making these souls suffer by keeping them here. I mean, how fucking demented are you to keep the dead away from peace?"

Juliet turned back to the fire. "So, you can see them."

"Of course I can!" I said angrily. "But I knew what you were doing, and there was no way I was going to let you use me for that."

"Such a selfish girl, Antigone," Juliet whispered to the fire. Then she said to me, "Do you even realize that you could have saved her?"

"I did save her," I said fiercely. "I'm not the one who poisoned Tori and left her brother to keep her alive with ghosts!"

"It takes a certain formula to keep someone alive," said Juliet, as if she was teaching a spelling class. "We needed someone who could see ghosts, perceive the future, and Chime. I had hoped my sister would have a son, and by all rights, Leandra, I know you should have been born a boy. That is why we dealt with you delicately when we discovered your infatuation with Ms. Justinia."

"Delicately?" I said incredulously. The six dark weeks that had followed roared in my ears like a lion. "That was your idea of delicate? For fuck's sake, you don't know anything. I kissed her because I knew it would warble you out enough to send her away, and it fucking worked. You conveniently forget that Lester raped her; that doesn't bother you, but two girls kissing?" I waved my hands in the air. "Perish the thought! You degenerate."

"Oh, my dear," Juliet put her hand on my face, and I pulled away as far as I could. "Your poor mind has always been confused. I wish it had been different for you."

I pretended to look amazed. "I think that's the first time we've ever agreed on something."

"Tori—"

"Tori won't ever be what you want," I said loudly. "You'll never be able to reach her."

"Perhaps, but she will find herself and become who she is destined to be when she reads this." Juliet held up the black book. "And you, my dear, are going to end all this kerfuffle and tell me where she is now."

I shook my head. "Nope."

Juliet shrugged. "Very well." She pulled a cellphone out of her pocket. My heart dropped when I saw the bright purple case with flowers; it was Olivia's phone.

"My my, she does have a lot of messages," said Juliet. "It's amazing what people will tell you when they think you're their mother." She looked back down at the phone. "Timothy Meadowlark," she said in a singsong voice. "Born of a Seer, related to one who can see ghosts, and drumming on pans like a Chime. Well, if he doesn't look like a fine candidate."

"Give me that," I said, trying to sound annoyed and not terrified about what Juliet had planned for the young child. My attempt to stand ended with me flat on my back. I did not feel well at all. Upside down, I watched Juliet look at the phone.

"We'll have to bring him here. He is like smoke," said Juliet quietly. She looked down at me. "For all your knowledge, Leandra, you have always lacked the ability to comprehend the greater picture. I wonder what your mother would think of you?"

"I bet it's better than what she thinks of you." I laughed. "But then, you can't see the ghosts very well," I shrugged, "so I guess you'll never know."

"Little snipe," Juliet hissed.

"Grow up, auntie," I said, being careful to keep my foot tapping in a consistent rhythm. "This isn't your game anymore."

She sent the ghosts at me again. It felt like my mind was seeing every movie ever made at once. Images, sounds, and rushes of emotions flooded my senses. It filled my reality until I couldn't tell if I was breathing or not. It felt like a bad dream, and I didn't know how to wake up.

The phenomena stopped, and I coughed, trying to find a breathing rhythm again. It took me a few moments to reorient myself. The ghosts tried to help me sit up.

My body hurt from falling down the stairs and fighting with Bjorn, but the ghosts had saved me from being severely injured in the fall. I was nauseous, but slowly regaining my stability.

"Juliet," I said breathily. I had to buy more time, wait for the ambulances and sheriff's deputies to arrive. I could take Juliet, but she had a gun and I could hardly stand. I had to wait; I had to be precise. I looked up at her imploringly, trying my best to look weak and pathetic, which was easier than I'd have liked it to be. "Please tell me."

Juliet looked interested in my plea. I had to draw this out; what could I say? The question came without thinking, and I felt fear ripple through me as I asked it, because I already knew the answer. "Tell me you didn't kill her to get me to see ghosts?"

"Who?" Juliet inquired.

"My mother!" I shouted.

"Huh," Juliet retorted, "as if it were so simple."

"Simple?" I said quietly, realizing the weight of what she was saying. "Juliet, did you let her die?"

Juliet did not answer, and that was answer enough; a terrible confirmation I had secretly hoped was not true. I felt an emptiness fill my stomach, and a rage I could hardly contain. It was past a red haze; it was alert awareness. My body felt like vibrating glass; my breath was all that existed between seconds. I wanted to run, to fight, to scream, to break something, to shatter the world with my cries like glass.

Juliet raged at me before I could do any of those things, her face contorted in rage like the monster I knew she was.

"Tori is here, now, with us, and you can see her!" Juliet shouted with venom. She wrapped her bony hands around my neck. I grabbed them to pull them away, and though I was stronger than Juliet, she held on as if she had nothing to lose. I could tell it was taking her a tremendous effort not to strangle me. "If she is alive, who haunts me now? Huh?" she said desperately. I could feel the rings on her fingers digging into my neck. "Tell me where she is!" I could feel her hands shaking.

I laughed despite my broken ribs. "You spent your life making enemies and you're surprised that you're followed by a horde of angry ghosts?

"*Liar!*" Juliet shrieked, tightening her grip. "Where is she? Tell me or I will break your bones."

"No, you won't," I said hoarsely, and broke her grip around my neck when my forearm hit her elbows. I pushed her away with my leg and arm, a jujitsu move Beatrice had drilled into me. I nodded to the ceiling. "Look up."

I half smiled as she turned her face above her. The ghosts loomed all around us, holding onto me protectively. I could hardly see Juliet through the many ghosts that had put themselves between her and me. I remembered some of them from years ago. It was clear that they remembered me.

Having a body does help when you are trying to protect someone, but it's not necessary. Angry people are much the same as angry ghosts; the projection of their anger is a powerful thing. Juliet couldn't see ghosts very well, but I knew she could see them well enough to know they held no compassion for her.

I knew the lost story of the Meadowlarks. The ghosts of Winter Hill were not guests, they were prisoners. I knew what Juliet had done to them, and I didn't blame them for their hatred.

"Feel cold, auntie?" I said.

She looked around at the ghosts in alarm. She said something quietly in Latin, but the ghosts didn't move. She tried again, to no effect.

I laughed and shook my head. "You're a terrible Chime."

"What is this?" snapped Juliet. "What have you *done?*"

"They see you, Juliet," I said. "They aren't happy that you used them."

"Why won't they obey me?" she whispered.

I stood up slowly, with the help of the many ghosts. I tapped my hands on my pants like a marching drum.

Tadda tat tat tadadada tat tat.

I could see the ghosts, and they all nodded, swayed, and moved to the beat of the marching rhythm. Like the drummer boy on a battlefield, the rhythm was to give them direction. But instead of Juliet's disgusting attempts to promise them the sun, it was me saying, "This is wrong, I want to help, let's end this."

"What are they doing?" asked Juliet, backing up against the wall.

"Ghosts are people, Juliet. Given the choice, who did you think they'd choose?" I said.

"How is this possible?" said Juliet, "*Oboedieritis mihi manes!* Obey me!"

"The Chime isn't hard," I said tiredly. "You just never understood what it meant."

"Stop this!" demanded Juliet. She picked up the revolver, and it shook in her bony hand. "Silence them!"

"No," I said. "You'll have to shoot me."

"I will," she said, though her hands shook, and her finger would not go to the trigger. I half believed her, but I knew her better than that. She would never do something so direct, something that could bring blame squarely on her. I didn't want to die, but I was tired of being afraid. If I died, Juliet would go to prison. Bjorn would be free of her at last. I had abandoned him so many times; I wasn't going to abandon him again. As soon as I saw Bjorn at the lawyer's office that morning, I knew that today would be the reaping of my atonement. I was ready for it. I wanted it to be over.

I stared past the barrel of the gun, my eyes not quite able to focus. "You can't," I said like the smartass I am.

It is not a smart thing to say to someone pointing a gun at you.

"Tell me, now!" shouted Juliet, and her voice echoed throughout the house. "Where is Tori? What ghost torments me? Who is still here?"

"I am," whispered a familiar, threatening voice behind me.

The ghosts swarmed me. All I could see was grey; I heard jumbles of voices, then something like a gunshot. I couldn't breathe. I crumpled under the weight of ghosts.

Yvonne Meadowlark Rainier

"Leandra!" I ran down the stairs as fast as I could without slipping. Silis got to her first. He sniffed her face and cried. A group of ghosts was standing in a tight circle around her. They gave me wary looks as I approached. I ignored the bone-chilling feeling of walking through ghosts and checked on Leandra. She was unconscious, but breathing. A gun was on the floor nearby. Juliet was cowering by the fireplace, her face paper white.

Antigone sat in front of her.

"What did you do to Leandra?!" I shouted.

"I'm just trying to find her," sobbed Juliet, tears in her eyes.

"Her? Tori? What about your sons, you miserable hag?"

The roller-skating ghost bent down and looked at Leandra, then gave me a reassuring smile.

Antigone's ghost continued to stare at her sister. Her hands were folded in her lap. Her hair streamed out around her. She looked calm, patient, and sad.

"They let her go," Juliet spat tearfully, her makeup and hair a hopeless mess. "You never had a child. I cannot let her go."

"Don't let Tori go because you can," said Antigone with immense compassion. "Do it because she needs you to."

"I need her," breathed Juliet. "I'm her mother! I will always know what's best for her."

"Best for her is far away from us," said Antigone.

"There is no life for us out there," sobbed Juliet. "The world hates what we can do."

"There has always been a life for us out there," I said angrily. "You just go and live it!"

"You had help!" screamed Juliet. "There was no one there to help me, to help us!"

"We had plenty," said Antigone, reaching a ghostly hand out to touch her sister's knee. "We were foolish." "You don't know." Juliet was crying hysterically. "You don't know what it's like to be afraid, Antigone. I always looked out for you."

"No," said Antigone. "Leandra, Tori, Bjorn, Lester, and Gerald never should have been subjected to this."

"You know what terrible things they did to me!" sobbed Juliet, throwing her hand in front of her face.

"Who cares?" I snapped, unable to contain my anger. "You think you're the only person who has suffered? There are many more who suffered worse than you and still came out knowing that just because bad shit happened to you does not give you the right to hurt someone else, especially your children!"

Silis's ears perked toward the giant door at the end of the room, and a moment later, I heard sirens.

Leandra stirred and groaned.

Antigone turned to me and whispered, "Get Leandra out."

"She'll want to see you."

"No," said Antigone sadly. "Please, take her."

The roller-skating ghost nodded encouragingly. I draped Leandra's arm over my shoulder and dragged her over to the door. She almost walked on her own after a few steps. At the door, she asked, "What happened?"

She turned to look back, but I opened the door quickly. Mom and Gerald were running toward us through the snow. I pulled Leandra outside before she could look behind her. The roller-skating ghost smiled at Leandra. The door closed heavily behind us.

Silis barked and jumped on his hind legs to alert the sheriff's deputies.

I pulled Leandra higher on my arm. "It's over."

Leandra Meadowlark

To be a good person, you don't cause trouble. You be nice, even when people are being assholes. You don't add to what's wrong. That's the best thing you can do. It takes a lot of work. You can't usually save the world by being a big hero; you have to do it by being small, insignificant, and brave. Problem is, when you have to do big, brave, heroic things, you end up getting your ass handed to you, but afterward, everyone expects you to be fine because you're the hero. Heroes may survive crazy shit, but they still hurt from it. They are not the same afterward.

"What are you thinking about?" asked Yvonne. Olivia and Gerald were in the front seat of the Trooper; Gerald was driving. Gerald's Bronco didn't have enough gas to get back to Rockhouse, and the one available ambulance that had followed them to Winter Hill was taking Lester and Bjorn to the hospital. An EMT had deemed me fit enough to go to the hospital in a car.

Juliet had been arrested. We'd agreed to follow the patrol cars back to Rockhouse in the Trooper. Their lights flashed in front of us and behind us. Even though a drip of ibuprofen would have been wonderful, I was extremely relieved that I didn't have to ride back in a deputy's patrol car or an ambulance.

Yvonne and I were sprawled across the back seat, leaning against the windows. I was curled up across most of the seat. Yvonne stretched her legs across the floorboards. Silis had somehow coiled himself in between us.

I opened my eyes a fraction and looked at Yvonne skeptically.

"For serious, I won't mock you this time," said Yvonne.

I sat up a bit. "I was wondering how someone so insignificant could work so hard and hurt so much."

Yvonne patted my knee. "You're not insignificant."

I grumbled and rolled my eyes, too tired to tell her not to ask if she didn't want to know what I meant.

"I mean, you're filthy, and you're terrible at small talk, but you're definitely not insignificant." Yvonne grinned.

I laughed once, because it was funny.

In the front seat, Gerald relaxed a fraction. The only one who saw it was Olivia, but it was a visible release. He bit his knuckle. Olivia rubbed his arm, then shook her head regally and looked back out the window. The sun was just rising when they got to Rockhouse, and a fresh layer of snow was falling.

Some of us are not meant to be the Chime. Some are not meant to see or feel the presence of ghosts. I envy them. They get to live without the burden of death, without the burden of those we've left behind, who don't want to stay there. They get to live their lives we honor, they are the makers of dreams. Oh, how I envy the dreamers, they don't know it all ends like smoke.

- Egor Meadowlark, Meadowlark Book of Myths

Scrawled beneath in blue pen by Gerald Meadowlark:

BULLSHIT.

The Last Goodbye

Two Days Later, Rockhouse

Bjorn sat stiffly at the foot of his hospital bed, staring at the wall as if it was the only thing keeping him from falling into the sky. His dirty clothes were crumpled at the end of the bed, where he had pulled them off and left them. He hated the hospital gown, but he also hated his clothes. They felt filthy in more ways than the dirt and sweat that was on them.

The recovery floor was quiet and dark, as to be expected during the early hours of the morning. Though the sound of soft footsteps from the nurses and the methodic hum of passing cars was soothing, there was no chance Bjorn would be able to sleep. His IV stand stood stoically next to him, the only real nuisance in the way of him getting up. It seemed to be asking him, "Why won't you go?"

"I'd burn them," said Leandra from the doorway, nodding toward his clothes. Bjorn jumped. Her own IV stand was next to her, tubes protruding from under her coat sleeve. "That's what I did with my stuff from that place."

Leandra tossed him a plastic bag. Bjorn looked at it tiredly.

Leandra grabbed her IV stand and rolled it away from the door. "I'll be out here when you're ready to go."

Bjorn looked exhausted. "Go where?"

Leandra tapped her IV pole with her finger and closed his door.

Bjorn, alone again, looked down at the bag. He had to pull his IV stand closer and push the tubes around to open it properly.

There was a pair of sweatpants, a clean T-shirt, a zip-up sweatshirt, and a pair of slippers. Leandra had been wearing something similar. Bjorn rubbed his forehead and put the clothes on as quickly as his sore limbs and his IV tubes would allow. The slippers fit perfectly; Leandra had remembered his shoe size. The T-shirt didn't really work with the IV, but felt good across his back, sleeves pulled over his stiff shoulders.

She was waiting for him when he opened the door, pushing his IV stand. She half smiled and got up sorely.

Bjorn looked at her tiredly. "Why do you want to see her?"

Leandra looked down for a moment and smiled at his slippers. "They fit?"

Bjorn nodded.

Leandra couldn't seem to find anything to say, so she took his free arm and they both walked slowly to the elevators, a familiar embrace of wounds and moving on to whatever was next. They followed the signs to the ICU.

The nurses knew who they were and led them to Juliet's bed. The poison had done its job.

Bjorn was still recovering from ingesting a small bit.

They suspected it was the same poison that had killed Lester, who was dead before arriving at the hospital.

A police officer nodded to Leandra and Bjorn as they approached the bed. Juliet's face was gaunt and sunken, her hair flat and thin. She breathed through a respirator, and her eyes were closed.

Bjorn's shoulders shook. Leandra's face was unreadable. A nurse came by and closed the curtains to give them some privacy.

Bjorn sat down on a rolling doctor's stool next to Juliet. He stiffly scooted to the edge of the bed, like he had for a dozen dying people before. His eyes held all the things he wished he could say but didn't know how to. "What's it like," he said suddenly, looking up at Leandra, "to lose your mom?"

Leandra looked at Juliet, and her hand clenched on her IV pole. "Like your shield is gone."

Bjorn nodded several times and sniffed. There was a dark bruise on his jaw from their fight. "I don't want her to die, but I don't want her to live," he said through a tense throat. "Isn't that messed up? My own mother..." Bjorn wiped his nose and took a breath. The effort to continue talking somewhat calmly appeared to cost him much. "You know they sent me to a group home after you left? An awful place with dirty beds. Everyone asked me, wanted to know... How can you tell them? How can you tell them your mother is a monster?" Bjorn wiped his nose again. "That place shut down after I left. Conditions were too bad. But I was heartbroken, because it was the best home I'd ever had. How messed up is that? A place people protested to have demolished was better than where we were."

Leandra nodded. "Nobody understands, either."

"No," said Bjorn, smiling, but not from happiness. "They don't." He peered over at Leandra. "Why are you here?"

Leandra gestured to Juliet. "She's dying."

"Yeah, but why are you still here?" Bjorn repeated.

Leandra nodded at the ground. She pulled a phone from her pocket and sifted through some pages. She handed the phone to Bjorn, who took it hesitantly. "I owe you a phone and several birthday presents. You can keep it," she said.

Bjorn wasn't interested in the phone but the picture on the screen: a girl with curly black hair, wearing a green sundress, purple leggings, and blue sneakers. She was smiling happily into the camera next to a giant sculpture of flowers.

Bjorn's face went blank.

"It's Tori," said Leandra, running her hand through her mess of dark hair. "She's safe."

Juliet gargled something without opening her eyes. A machine started to beep, a nurse came from behind the curtain and examined her, then looked earnestly at the two cousins, said, "Not much time now." She turned off the machine and left them once more.

Bjorn pulled his stool closer to the bed and pulled his IV tubes up. He put the picture of Tori in front of his mother's closed eyes. "There's Tori, Mom," Bjorn said in barely a whisper. "She's beautiful."

Leandra left to sit in the hallway. It was more difficult to walk on her own, but she managed.

When Bjorn came out a little while later, holding the phone tightly, Leandra got up and they hobbled back to their rooms together.

Before they parted for their separate rooms, Bjorn asked, "Will you Chime for her?"

Leandra shook her head sadly, "I can't. It has to be…meant. I don't think I ever could…for her."

Bjorn nodded in something like agreement. "Do you have a place to go?" He half smiled. "After all this?"

"Yeah," said Leandra. "You?"

Bjorn nodded. "Yeah. I didn't mean to stay this long."

"I got your number," Leandra pointed to the phone. "Keep in touch."

Bjorn half smiled again. "It might not be a lot."

"I understand," said Leandra. "Just let me know you're alive, and call me if you need me." She tried to smile for real. "No one gets to kick your ass but me."

Bjorn did smile for real, and he looked like a kid again, just for a second. He walked his IV stand down the hall, then stopped. "Leandra, if you see Tori…"

"She says hi," said Leandra. "She doesn't hate you, and she hopes she can see you sometime. Her number is in the phone."

Bjorn looked shocked, then looked down at the phone, where a text alert appeared from a contact called "Tori."

Hi, today sucks. Hope u feel better soon! Call me!! <3 Sis

"I totally lied to you guys, by the way," said Leandra. "I never found her; she found me."

Bjorn nodded, stifling sadness and joy. "See you, Leandra."

"Later, Bjorn."

The final reality is that a Chime is for the living. It does not matter if you see ghosts or know the future. The job of a Chime is to fill the holes in hearts, to shine lights into the caverns and expose the darkest shadows. We are the unwanted and the wanted, the needed and the hated. We don't have shorter lives, we are just more easily forgotten. The point of our work is to be forgotten. We are like the sand on the beach; filling the holes made by footprints, to make it new for someone else.

- Leandra's notes, Meadowlark Book of Myths

The Chime

Leandra Meadowlark

I had every meteorite that could be found brought back to me at the house. Deputy Martinez delivered them himself. I met him a few days after the incident and shook his hand. He said I was taller now, and held out one of my self-produced albums for me to sign.

"Keep in touch, Leandra," he said before leaving.

I spent that first night home from the hospital with the meteorites at the kitchen table downstairs. By early morning, the house and property were swarming with curious ghosts.

Dad, Martin, and Yvonne helped me take the meteorites out to the field behind Beatrice's house, where we dispersed them in no particular fashion.

All the ghosts had come from Winter Hill and were wandering about the meteorites in the field.

I had one piece of meteorite on a string around my neck, and the ghosts that were drawn to it all stood around me, looking curiously at it.

There was one ghost I wanted most to see, and I knew she wasn't there.

"This isn't how you're going to find her, kid," said the ghost of Beatrice. I turned and saw her standing next to me, giving me the same old condescending look through her half-closed eyes. She was shorter than I, but dwarfed me. She looked more solid than the others. "She's not here."

"How are you here?" I said. "I Chimed for you!"

"Yeah, but you didn't mean it," said Beatrice tartly. "You didn't want me to go."

"I'll never want you to go," I said indignantly.

The ghost of my former babysitter punched me on the shoulder appreciatively. Her hand went right through me. "That's my girl."

I smiled at her, but I had to know. "How do you know she's not here?"

"I looked," said Beatrice, almost offended that I had to ask. Then she said, "No time to waste, girl. It's time for all of us to go."

I looked away.

"You did get me a bit extra as a ghost," said Beatrice. "That's not quite fair to everyone else, is it?"

I rubbed my nose. "None of this is fair."

Beatrice nodded. "That's true. But it's my time, deario. I don't want to lose more of myself than I already have. And you got places to go and a life to live. You need to leave all of this behind. Chime for us, will you?"

I nodded and took a few deep breaths. The early dawn lit up the fields in yellows and reds that glittered against the frosty brush. The hundreds of ghosts milling around the meteorites looked colorful in the light, twinkling like mist.

The harmonica smelled familiarly of reeds. It felt comfortable in my hand. I took another deep breath, stalling. "What do you want to hear?"

"You know the one." Beatrice winked.

I fingered the old harmonica. "You saved me," I told Beatrice. "After all that was done, you're the one that saved me."

"Likewise, deario," said Beatrice, walking down the lawn to join the others in the field. "Now, Chime your heart out."

Yvonne Meadowlark Rainier

I sat on the roof of Martin's house with Gerald, watching Leandra in the yard. Mom and Martin were in the warm house, but I wanted to see it from the outside without being in the way. It was crazy to see so many ghosts in one place. Leandra stood alone, looking down the field stoically, holding the harmonica in her hand and tapping her fingers, as if she was waiting for a conductor to signal the orchestra to begin.

"I had a hard time getting four ghosts to cross," I said quietly to Gerald. "You think she can make them all go?"

Gerald smiled, and he looked boyish. He must have been very young when he married Antigone. "Definitely," he said.

We both waited in silence.

Leandra Meadowlark

I waited for the red sun to hit the top of the distant hills. I waited for the reflection to glow into the fields. I waited for the spark of curiosity in the eyes of all the ghosts gathered around me. I waited until they were ready.

Then I began the Chime.

I started by tapping my heel on a cement block below my foot. It was a deep, definitive sound.

Thump, thump-thump, thump, thump-thump.

Keeping with the rhythm, I began with one long, low note on the harmonica. It was the note of melancholy; recognition that death generally sucks and there isn't much you can do about it. This gets their attention, as most all of the ghosts still around are tuned to this frequency.

I switched to a few notes of turmoil, vibrating across my lips and into the cold morning air. My breath hitched a few times, as it hurt to breathe in, but the ghosts nodded back and forth, following the rhythm. It was a riff I often played on my own. It was long and melodic and clear; a song for the people. The ghosts began to sway.

It doesn't matter what song the Chime chooses to play, because ghosts don't hear the tune; they hear the truth in it. Music carries meaning that language can't communicate. It's the one sure way for a ghost to truly hear you. I had to pick a song I knew I could play and not feel afraid, or they would be afraid, as most of them had been so afraid already.

I continued to drum on the ground.

Thump, thump-thump, thump, thump-thump.

The riff melded seamlessly into the Chime as I played out a long, clear rhythm. I hate playing it in front of other people because it's painfully clichéd, and people have all these other meanings that they read into it, but it's my song, the song that makes me believe. In my head, I heard the words as I played in my own musical voice:

> I once was lost
> *Thump, thump-thump,*
> but now I'm found
> *Thump, thump-thump*

Tones danced and sang through vibrating soundwaves; crescendos and arches left my fingers tingling. Notes were added, but the tune remained the same. My body moved to the beat of the line.

> *Thump, thump-thump, thump, thump-thump.*
> Was blind
> *Thump, thump-thump,*
> but now
> *Thump thump,*
> I see.

One by one, the ghosts started to step forward, hearing a calling, seeing the rising sun, comforted by the presence of the meteors they had originally followed, and elated at the sight of their one true star. I played with all my strength. As long as they were moving, they would hear, and they would go. They would understand the truth, see the light, and know it was time to leave.

Yvonne Meadowlark Rainier

I had not bawled my eyes out so much since the night I saw Richard cross over. It was such a powerful scene. Leandra played that harmonica beautifully. If I wasn't watching with my own eyes, I'd have thought she was playing with a symphony. I would never have believed something so pure and real could come out of a little box of reeds, or that my quiet cousin could be the one to deliver the Chime so perfectly. But there she was, echoing her song down the grounds, all across the fields of Rockhouse, with pristine clarity. The ghosts looked up, one by one, and stepped into the sun, disappearing into the dawn like smoke.

Leandra ended on one long, low note; the sound gently faded into the breeze rustling the brush of the fields. She opened her eyes slowly and looked out across the familiar ground.

The wind rustled across the yellow brush of the empty field like the crescendo of a passing car.

Woooooooshooooooo.

Meeting the Meadowlarks

"You're an illustrator?" asked Leandra inquisitively. After putting her bag down on the floor, she picked up one of the drawings I had been working on. I clicked the lights on as Silis walked in and shook happily. It felt really good to be home.

"Well, sort of. I'm doing freelance work for some people I know. It's kinda hard to get into the business of straight freelance," I mumbled, putting a bag of groceries on the counter.

Leandra gave me a funny look.

"What?" I said incredulously.

"Nothing."

"What?"

"Everything is hard." Leandra put the drawing of the turtle back down and limped over to the kitchen. Her foot was in a large medical boot thanks to her fall down the stairs. Silis followed her as she opened the cupboards and poured herself a bowl of cereal.

My phone beeped before I could reply. "Grandma Lilly wants us to come over." I looked up at the wall clock. It was noon. We decided to stay the night in a hotel instead of driving straight back home over the mountains. I still wanted to sleep, but I didn't want to keep Grandma Lilly waiting.

"We should go, then," said Leandra shortly, putting the empty cereal bowl in the sink.

"Jeez, did you inhale that?" I asked.

Leandra raised an eyebrow as she pulled her tablet from her backpack and went out to the car.

I looked over and at my empty box of cereal.

"Silis, my new roomie is a serial cereal eater. Haaaa."

I took a bite out of my giant piece of banana bread and nodded in satisfaction. "Is it wrong that I feel so good about being better than Juliet?"

"Superiority isn't always a sin, my dear," said Grandma Lilly, sitting on her old, floral sofa with a cup of tea. Leandra was sitting on the stairs in the other room, leaning against the wall. It was a sunny spot. Mom and I were at the bar counter. I was shamelessly stuffing my face with the fresh loaf of banana bread on the counter.

"Feel free to take comfort that you will never lead such a wretched life," said Mom, sipping tea whilst reading her latest paperback. The cover of this one featured a man in a suit, holding a gun, a damsel in a red dress on his arm. Mom had moved on to pulp spy adventures.

Grandma Lilly raised her teaspoon in the air. "As the great poet says, 'You have principles for purpose, courage to save you, and valor in strife.' There will come a time when we all face the sun, and as you have seen, many times, there are some of us who stay for reasons their heart did not fulfill." Grandma Lilly nodded knowingly. "Be proud of your valiant heart, and live a life so bright only the sun can take you."

Leandra smiled, sitting on the stairs, out of eyesight of everyone.

A valiant heart. Did she have a valiant heart?

Janet came in the front door with baby Tim in his front-pack and her husband Mark in tow. "Where's Leandra?" she said breathily. Yvonne pointed up the stairs. Leandra stood up quickly. Janis ran up the stairs so enthusiastically that she almost ran into her.

"Leandra!" said Janis, giving her a fierce side-hug and a kiss on the cheek. "Thank you so much for helping Yvonne and Timmy! I appreciate it so much! Also, I Saw you at the college tomorrow, but you must wear a different shirt. It's going to be a much fancier occasion than you think!"

Leandra tilted her head in confusion.

"Here," Janis said, handing her a folded stack of shirts and a fresh pair of jeans. "There are some shirts of mine. You can have them for school and jobs. You'll be able to get your own soon, but you should have some new ones for your meeting with the professors tomorrow. They're going to want to have dinner with you because of your work on your music theory thesis."

Leandra looked over at me.

I toasted her with my banana bread. This was what it was like growing up with family who could see the future.

Janis sorted through the clothes pile happily but stopped in horror at a dark red shirt folded beneath a black one. "AH! Oh Mark, this is the shirt!"

Leandra snatched it before she could take it back and put it under her arm. "This is my favorite color."

Yvonne and Mom laughed as Janis followed Leandra up the stairs, insisting that Leandra wear the blue one or the black one.

"I like her." Grandma Lilly waved her spoon in the air. "She chose the better way."

"What's the better way?" I inquired, passing Mark the butter for the pumpkin bread.

"The hardest one imaginable," said Grandma Lilly. "Forgiving the terrible and expressing the wonderful." She sipped her tea and chortled. "By the light, we cannot see."

Leandra came down the stairs wearing the dark red shirt Janet found so offensive. She put on her sunglasses and posed like a superhero. Janis shook her head in defeat. Timmy blew bubbles with spit.

"Wonderful," said Grandma Lilly approvingly.

HEROES

Yvonne Meadowlark Rainier

"So, what do you want to do?" I asked, pawing through the grocery bag on the kitchen counter. We had gotten back late. I still had to clean out the back room for Leandra.

Leandra sat down on the couch and closed her eyes. "I want to sleep."

"Well, you can crash on the couch, or we can move all the stuff in the back room out here and deal with that tomorrow."

"Hm," said Leandra.

"Yeah," I said, looking at the mess of the house. It was a catastrophe to begin with, and I already knew I'd have to get rid of a bunch of stuff. The empty sack of burrito wrappers was still on the table. It was a good opportunity to clean things up.

"Which room is it?" said Leandra.

"Back room on the right." I pointed and grimaced. "We'll have to put the guitars in my room."

"Guitars?" Leandra raised an eyebrow, "You play?"

"Terribly. Richard played; they were his. My niece Stephanie has been learning to play. She uses the back room to practice sometimes."

"Mind if I look?" said Leandra.

I grabbed a bottle of water and waved down the hallway. "Let's go."

The room was cleaner than the rest of the house, but that's because it had been Richard's music room, and I made an effort to keep it nice. Guitars hung from hooks on the walls. The futon we used for guests was in the corner.

"We can find you a real bed tomorrow," I said.

"I like the futon," said Leandra, nodding approvingly at the walls. "The guitars can stay, if that's all right with you."

"There's, like, no room left for you," I said.

Leandra put her backpack on the ground, her tablet on Richard's empty drafting table, and her harmonica on top of it. She looked around inquisitively. "Might need a bookshelf."

I shrugged. "There's a free one on Craigslist every week."

"It's all good, then," said Leandra, testing the door handle.

I shrugged. "OK, then. Did you want the books in here?" I asked, nodding down the hallway to the cardboard box of books from Winter Hill.

Leandra looked at them, considering. "I'll take a look."

"Okey dokey. You want a burrito?"

"In a bit," said Leandra.

I went to the back porch to let Silis out. The porch light was buzzing loudly, and I hated leaving it on. I knew it was going to burn out soon and coaxed Silis to hurry up so I could turn it off.

I turned when I heard the sound of books falling over. Leandra was pulling books out of the box at an alarming rate.

"Where's the book?" she asked frantically.

"What book?" I said.

"THE book, the only book that fucking mattered! Where is it?" stormed Leandra, throwing books across the room. Silis barked.

"HEY!" I shouted, closing the slider door quickly. "Calm down."

Leandra kicked the box aside and fell against the wall. "It's all that's left."

"Of what?" I exclaimed, looking at the pile of books scattered across the ground.

"Mom and Tori!" Leandra shouted. "It's the book I read her, it's gone. Juliet took it! It's—" Leandra's face contorted into grief. She clenched her fists and inhaled sharply, fighting back sobs so hard she could barely breathe. She slid down the wall to the ground, gasping. Her hands clenched in her hair.

Silis whined and went to lick her face. I held onto his collar to keep him from completely bombarding her.

"*Fuck*," she cried. "I'm sorry."

"No, it's OK," I said, sitting down on the floor across from her. "Why is it so important?"

Leandra covered her mouth with the back of her thumb and looked at me with her bright honey-colored eyes. She suddenly looked like the little child I remembered from the family reunion.

She stretched her jaw. "It was our book," she said, "me, Tori, and...Mom."

Her face crumpled into sadness, and she began to sob. Her shoulders shook. Silis whined. I looked back at the couch, pulled off the blanket and a few pillows, and grabbed a tissue box. I sat down next to Leandra and put the blanket over her knees. I put a pillow next to her and set the tissue box down. Silis came and sat in my lap, looking up at me worriedly. I had never sat against that particular wall before. I had certainly gotten familiar with sitting and crying in various parts of the house, but not in this one.

This one must be Leandra's spot.

I held out the tissue box to Leandra. She took several and wiped her face. She took some deep breaths to stop crying. She held her forehead with tense fingers and stared off into the distance. Her face was red and completely wet.

"It sucks," I said at last, pulling the pillow behind my back, "and no matter what people say, it doesn't really get better."

Leandra scrunched her eyes shut and took a hard breath in.

"I got a whole closet of tissues, three quarts of ice cream in the fridge, and a very worried dog who cares a lot about you," I said, and on cue, Silis pawed away from my hands and sniffed at Leandra's face worriedly. "Tell me."

"What?" said Leandra.

"It," I said. "All of it."

I sat in silence, petting Silis, feeling the strange familiarity of sitting on the floor and experiencing the full force of grief. It was dark out, and the porch light was still on, but it could wait. There was no hurry.

After a long silence, Leandra swallowed and said, "She wasn't supposed to die."

I nodded at the wall in front of me, sighing in mutual frustration. "And that's the fucking shit of it."

Several hours later, we were both numb from sitting on the floor, and Silis had fallen asleep. We decided that the couch would be a better place to sit; I helped Leandra up after falling over since my butt was numb. We laughed at ourselves and hobbled over to the couch. Leandra flopped down, and I went to turn off the porch light.

"You want vanilla, mint chocolate chip, or peanut butter chocolate?" I asked.

"Which one do you want?" she asked.

"Don't care."

"Mint chocolate chip."

I grabbed the quart of mint chocolate chip and the peanut butter for myself. I also pulled four water bottles from the package by the front door. Silis was trying to follow Leandra into the bathroom.

"You want to watch a movie?" I asked.

"Sure. You're not tired?"

"It's 4 a.m. It's already tomorrow," I said, putting the ice cream and spoons on the table. "I want to watch a space movie. You seen the ones with laser-sword fighting?"

"Cha," scoffed Leandra. "I lived with a cult, not under a rock."

"Which one?"

"How about the second one?"

"What, like, the one with the clones?" I said with disgust.

"No, the good one. We had standards."

"OK, I was almost going to have to kick you out for a second."

"Fair enough."

I fiddled with the TV remotes and channels while Leandra was in the bathroom. My copies of the movies were on VHS, so I had to switch around cables. By the time Leandra got back, the previews were half over and I was a quarter-way through my ice cream. OK, maybe a third, but not, like, half. Yet.

I held up a spoon that she took without looking away from the TV. Silis would have licked it otherwise.

I'm not going to say it was fun, because dealing with shit like that is never fun. But sitting back and just having someone who will eat a quart of ice cream with you and watch a movie at four in the morning because you are too emotionally drained to sleep?

It helps.

Leandra Meadowlark

I never slept until Tori and Mom were asleep. After Tori left, I don't think I slept much at all.

I never wanted to die, but it didn't seem like I'd have much of a choice. I didn't have a family that could help me. To me, family was something that could only help from far away, or something that could hardly help at all.

I don't hate my dad for not doing more; I hate the world for not listening to him.

I don't hate my mom for the choices she made; I hate the people who made her afraid.

I kept my world to myself, because no one was there to help me when they should have.

I'd had boxes of angry poetry, terrible stories, songs, dreams of places I would never go. Beatrice and I had burned them in the backyard, right before I went off to college, and it had been liberating.

"Winter Hill is not who you are," Beatrice had told me through the smoke. "You are who you are, and if you make any excuses otherwise, I'll come over those mountains, hell or high water, and wipe the floor with you."

My favorite part of Winter Hill, if there could be one, was that time before I fell asleep and the manor was quiet. Mom, Tori, and I shared a bed, and I always fell asleep last. Sometimes Mom let us leave the light on for a bit, and I read Tori stories in whispers from a stack of books beside the bed.

There was always that one book; I must have read it two hundred times, but I can't for the life of me remember what it was about or how it ended, besides the weird image of a monk and a traveler sitting together in a temple, watching the smoke from a candle burn. They must have been talking about heroes, because I remember Tori asking me about it quietly, in the near dark when the rest of the world seemed so quiet.

"Do you think there are heroes like that out there?" Tori asked tiredly, her head resting on my shoulder. My arm had gone numb from her weight a long time before, but I knew I could move her gently away when she was asleep.

"I don't know," I said. "I bet we could find them someday."

"That'd be fun," Tori said drowsily. "I want to be a hero," she said, and soon she was fast asleep.

When Mom and Tori slept, I would sit awake for a while, listening, until all the sounds of the manor stilled, and I knew there was no threat to our small time of peace. In those minutes of seclusion and security, I felt like I had the world to myself. I would lie awake and dream of places far from Winter Hill, where I could take Tori and Mom and be safe and read books. In those stories, I was the hero, and I would save them.

Even though I couldn't do it all in real life, in my mind, I could be enough for just one moment, and that kept me going through to the next day, when I could look forward to being a hero for a few moments once again.

Funny thing is, there's not that large of a step between believing something and it coming true.

Years later, I realized that I was really saving myself, and I felt ashamed about it. I told Beatrice that once when she asked me what was up.

She nodded knowingly. "You can't save anyone if you don't save yourself first," she said. I searched her face for disapproval, but there was only a grim look of wisdom. "You were the hero, Leandra, because you saved yourself. Most don't understand that that's the hardest thing of all."

Even at Beatrice's house with Dad, I wouldn't fall asleep until the house was silent and everyone else was asleep, because I knew it was only then that I was safe to dream. In those long minutes of silence, safe from my own thoughts and those of others, I could dare to be something greater than myself.

I could be the hero.

Yvonne Meadowlark Rainier

Halfway through the movie, Silis started licking Leandra's cardboard ice cream carton. I pulled it out of the dog's reach and put it on the table. I let Silis lick the spoon, though, because most of the ice cream was gone anyway. I put the lid on the carton and turned the movie's volume down to almost zero. It was just starting to get lighter outside. Leandra was dead asleep. I put my feet up on the other side of the couch, and Silis settled himself comfortably on the floor below. I wasn't going to be awake much longer, but I had to see the cloud city and Luke making that weird face when he screams "*No!*" because that's exactly what we felt like doing, too.

Found

Three Months Later, Long Tree Storage, Rockhouse

"I found the key in her safe," said Martin, holding out the key to the storage unit. "You ready?

Leandra took the key. On a little yellow tag tied to it was scrawled, in Beatrice's handwriting, "Leandra."

"Not really," said Leandra, turning the key over in her hands.

Martin smiled. "Whatever's in there is yours."

"Kind of exciting," said Yvonne, holding Silis's leash. "You know, like opening a treasure vault or something. Also, tax free!"

Leandra nodded and unlatched the lock of the storage unit. Everyone held their breath as the lock fell to the ground and Leandra pulled open the door.

The dust settled quickly, and everyone was speechless as Leandra walked slowly around her inheritance.

Martin chuckled. "I knew she didn't sell it."

"Is that a Ural?" asked Yvonne, admiring the pristine, if dusty, Russian motorcycle with a sidecar parked neatly in the compartment.

Leandra nodded. "It is."

"Does it start?" asked Martin excitedly.

Leandra found the ignition; the key was inside it. The bike turned over and hummed like a drumroll.

Ra da da da da da da.

"I always wondered why she made me get my motorcycle endorsement," Leandra said, "Ugh, I failed it twice, and she wouldn't give me my driver's license until I passed it."

"Nice," said Yvonne, checking out the dark green paint job as Martin checked over the mechanics. "It'll fit right in with the Fleetwood."

Across the freeway, sitting on top of a 1990 Subaru Outback, a girl lowered her binoculars and smiled. The radio buzzed playful music from the old stereo. She knew she wouldn't be staying long, so she wasn't worried about her battery going dead.

She tapped her multicolored nails on her car roof and took out her phone. She snapped a picture of Leandra through the lens of the binoculars.

Leandra looked a lot like she remembered.

"Found you," said Tori cheerfully.

A grey ghost sat next to her on the roof, her long skirt flaring out as she swung her roller-skate-clad feet cheerfully. She blew a bubble of grey bubble gum.

Tori turned to the ghost next to her. "Ready to go?"

The ghost responded by sliding off the car roof, being mindful of her skirt, and skating round to the passenger's seat, which she got into without opening the door.

Tori Harrow looked back one last time at her cousin. Her eyes, catching the spring sunlight, were a beautiful honey yellow. "See you in no time."

Leandra looked up across the highway. She thought for a moment that she saw someone she recognized, but she must have imagined it. Yvonne scolded Silis for happily jumping into the sidecar.

They cheered at the spectacle as Martin rode through the storage facility's alleys with Silis in the sidecar. Leandra laughed in happiness, and the familiar face from across the highway vanished from her mind like smoke.

Thank you to the original Kickstarter backers, without whom, this would just be a collection of lost ghosts.

Peter Marinari · Grace · Heather M. Harkins · Dustin Fanning-Painter · Belinda · Lara Milton, Editor Extraordinaire · Jean Chretien · Kat and Jesse · Jessie · S.L. Puma · Molly Griffin · Holly Steele · Woody Arnold · Shannon Brown · Protector Dragon · Zarina Rebecca Bell · Abital & Daryl · Kayla Stokes · Christopher Deel · Jenny P · Akurol · JamesChats · Peggy Somerville · Twinka & Tuky Lupher · LaVonne Bohning

The Meadowlark Saga will continue in
Like Smoke

www.ingramcontent.com/pod-product-compliance
Lightning Source LLC
Chambersburg PA
CBHW022003170726
47994CB00022B/1884